# JULIUS CAESAR

## *WITH READER'S GUIDE*

## AMSCO LITERATURE PROGRAM

WILBERT J. LEVY, *Program Editor*

*William Shakespeare*

# JULIUS CAESAR

*Amsco Literature Program*

*When ordering this book, you may specify:*
R 86 ALP *(Paperback)*
R 86 H *(Hardbound)*

# WITH READER'S GUIDE

*Helene Cunningham*

*Formerly Teacher of English*
*Newtown High School, New York City*

*Amsco School Publications, Inc.*
315 HUDSON STREET NEW YORK, N.Y. 10013

ISBN 0-87720-802-6 (Paperback)
ISBN 0-87720-834-4 (Hardbound)

Julius Cæsar with Reader's Guide

The text of JULIUS CÆSAR is that of The Aldus Shakespeare, published by arrangement with Funk & Wagnalls, New York. All rights reserved.

Amsco School Publications, Inc.

Printed in the United States of America

# CONTENTS

Julius Cæsar                                           3
Reader's Guide
    Introduction                  215
    Questions                     225

## Characters in the Play

Julius Cæsar
Octavius Cæsar ⎫
Mark Antony ⎬ triumvirs after the death of Julius Cæsar
Lepidus ⎭
Cicero ⎫
Publius ⎬ senators
Popilius Lena ⎭
Marcus Brutus ⎫
Cassius ⎪
Casca ⎪
Trebonius ⎪
Ligarius ⎬ conspirators against Julius Cæsar
Decius Brutus ⎪
Metellus Cimber ⎪
Cinna ⎭
Flavius and Marullus, tribunes
Artemidorus of Cnidos, a teacher of rhetoric
A Soothsayer
Cinna, a poet
Another Poet
Lucilius ⎫
Titinius ⎪
Messala ⎬ friends to Brutus and Cassius
Young Cato ⎪
Volumnius ⎭
Varro ⎫
Clitus ⎪
Claudius ⎬ servants to Brutus
Strato ⎪
Lucius ⎭
Dardanius
Pindarus, servant to Cassius

Calpurnia, wife to Cæsar
Portia, wife to Brutus

Senators, Citizens, Guards, Attendants, &c

*The Tragedy of Julius Caesar*

3 **being mechanical**   being people of the working class.

11 **cobbler**   this word had two meanings: "one who mends shoes" and "clumsy workman."

15 **naughty**   wicked, good for nothing.
**knave**   manservant or worker of low position; meant insultingly in this case.

# ACT I

*Scene 1. Rome. A street*

*Enter Flavius, Marullus, and certain Commoners.*

**Flavius**
Hence! home, you idle creatures, get you home:
Is this a holiday? what! know you not,
Being mechanical, you ought not walk
Upon a laboring day without the sign
Of your profession? Speak, what trade art thou?          5

**First Commoner**
Why, sir, a carpenter.

**Marullus**
Where is thy leather apron and thy rule?
What dost thou with thy best apparel on?
You, sir, what trade are you?

**Second Commoner**
Truly, sir, in respect of a fine workman, I am but,          10
as you would say, a cobbler.

**Marullus**
But what trade art thou? answer me directly.

**Second Commoner**
A trade, sir, that, I hope, I may use with a safe con-
science; which is indeed, sir, a mender of bad soles.

**Marullus**
What trade, thou knave? thou naughty knave, what
    trade?          15

3

21 **awl**   pointed instrument for punching holes in leather.


25 **neats-leather**   cowhide.


33 **tributaries**   those who pay tribute.

*Second Commoner*

Nay, I beseech you, sir, be not out with me: yet, if
you be out, sir, I can mend you.

*Marullus*

What mean'st thou by that? mend me, thou saucy
    fellow!

*Second Commoner*

Why, sir, cobble you.

*Flavius*

Thou art a cobbler, art thou?                               20

*Second Commoner*

Truly, sir, all that I live by is with the awl: I meddle
with no tradesman's matters, nor women's matters,
but with awl. I am indeed, sir, a surgeon to old shoes;
when they are in great danger, I re-cover them. As
proper men as ever trod upon neats-leather have gone   25
upon my handiwork.

*Flavius*

But wherefore art not in thy shop today?
Why dost thou lead these men about the streets?

*Second Commoner*

Truly, sir, to wear out their shoes, to get myself into
more work. But indeed, sir, we make holiday, to see   30
Cæsar and to rejoice in his triumph.

*Marullus*

Wherefore rejoice? What conquest brings he home?
What tributaries follow him to Rome,
To grace in captive bonds his chariot-wheels?
You blocks, you stones, you worse than senseless
    things!                                               35
O you hard hearts, you cruel men of Rome,
Knew you not Pompey? Many a time and oft
Have you climb'd up to walls and battlements,
To towers and windows, yea, to chimney-tops,
Your infants in your arms, and there have sat          40

46 **replication** echo.

49 **cull out** choose

51 **Pompey's blood** Cæsar had just defeated Pompey's two sons in Spain.

54 **intermit** suspend.

58 **Tiber banks** the banks of Rome's river.

60 **most exalted shores** the highest point on its banks to which the river had ever risen.

61 **basest metal** the lowest nature among them.

65 **ceremonies** wreaths, scarfs, or garlands.

67 **Lupercal** the feast of a god of fertility. Actually Cæsar's triumphant return to Rome had occurred the preceding October and this feast took place on February 15. For dramatic intensity, Shakespeare combined the two events and even moved the Lupercal forward into the month of March.

The live-long day with patient expectation
To see great Pompey pass the streets of Rome:
And when you saw his chariot but appear,
Have you not made an universal shout,
That Tiber trembled underneath her banks          45
To hear the replication of your sounds
Made in her concave shores?
And do you now put on your best attire?
And do you now cull out a holiday?
And do you now strew flowers in his way            50
That comes in triumph over Pompey's blood?
Be gone!
Run to your houses, fall upon your knees,
Pray to the gods to intermit the plague
That needs must light on this ingratitude.         55

*Flavius*

Go, go, good countrymen, and, for this fault,
Assemble all the poor men of your sort;
Draw them to Tiber banks and weep your tears
Into the channel, till the lowest stream
Do kiss the most exalted shores of all.            60

             [*Exeunt all the Commoners.*

See, whether their basest metal be not mov'd;
They vanish tongue-tied in their guiltiness.
Go you down that way towards the Capitol;
This way will I: disrobe the images,
If you do find them deck'd with ceremonies.        65

*Marullus*

May we do so?
You know it is the feast of Lupercal.

*Flavius*

It is no matter; let no images
Be hung with Cæsar's trophies. I'll about,
And drive away the vulgar from the streets:        70
So do you too, where you perceive them thick.
These growing feathers pluck'd from Cæsar's wing

73 **ordinary pitch**   normal flight.


**Exeunt**   they leave.


Stage directions **Flourish**   fanfare of trumpets.


6 **course**   the traditional race on the Lupercal had originally
been run by the priests who went about among the people
striking at them with leather thongs as a token of purifica-
tion. Later, young men of good family, like Antony, took
up the custom as a sport.

Will make him fly an ordinary pitch,
Who else would soar above the view of men
And keep us all in servile fearfulness.                    75

                              [*Exeunt.*


## Scene 2. A *public place*

*Flourish. Enter Cæsar; Antony, for the course; Cal-*
*purnia, Portia, Decius, Cicero, Brutus, Cassius, and*
*Casca; a great crowd following, among them a*
*Soothsayer.*

*Cæsar*
  Calpurnia!
*Casca*
            Peace, ho! Cæsar speaks.
                              [*Music ceases.*
*Cæsar*
                              Calpurnia!
*Calpurnia*
  Here, my lord.
*Cæsar*
  Stand you directly in Antonius' way,                     5
  When he doth run his course. Antonius!
*Antony*
  Cæsar, my lord?
*Cæsar*
  Forget not, in your speed, Antonius,
  To touch Calpurnia; for our elders say,
  The barren, touched in this holy chase,                  10
  Shake off their sterile curse.
*Antony*
            I shall remember:
  When Cæsar says "do this," it is perform'd.

21 **ides of March**    March 15.

Stage directions **Sennet**    the sounding of a trumpet.

29 **order of the course**    running of the race.

Cæsar
  Set on, and leave no ceremony out.

                                        [Flourish.

Soothsayer
  Cæsar!                                                15
Cæsar
  Ha! who calls?
Casca
  Bid every noise be still: peace yet again!
Cæsar
  Who is it in the press that calls on me?
  I hear a tongue, shriller than all the music,
  Cry "Cæsar." Speak; Cæsar is turn'd to hear.       20
Soothsayer
  Beware the ides of March.
Cæsar
                        What man is that?
Brutus
  A soothsayer bids you beware the ides of March.
Cæsar
  Set him before me; let me see his face.
Cassius
  Fellow, come from the throng; look upon Cæsar.     25
Cæsar
  What say'st thou to me now? speak on again.
Soothsayer
  Beware the ides of March.
Cæsar
  He is a dreamer; let us leave him: pass.
            [Sennet. Exeunt all but Brutus and Cassius.
Cassius
  Will you go see the order of the course?
Brutus
  Not I.                                              30

32 **gamesome** lively, interested in sports.

38 **wont** used, accustomed.
39 **bear . . . hand** treat harshly and like a stranger.

45 **passions of some difference** conflicting feelings.

47 **give some soil** may affect.

50 **construe** interpret.

53 **passion** emotional condition.

59 **just** true.

*Cassius*

I pray you, do.

*Brutus*

I am not gamesome: I do lack some part
Of that quick spirit that is in Antony.
Let me not hinder, Cassius, your desires;
I'll leave you.　　　　　　　　　　　　　　　35

*Cassius*

Brutus, I do observe you now of late:
I have not from your eyes that gentleness
And show of love as I was wont to have:
You bear too stubborn and too strange a hand
Over your friend that loves you.　　　　　40

*Brutus*

　　　　　　　　　　　　Cassius,
Be not deceiv'd: if I have veil'd my look,
I turn the trouble of my countenance
Merely upon myself. Vexed I am
Of late with passions of some difference,　　45
Conceptions only proper to myself,
Which give some soil perhaps to my behaviors;
But let not therefore my good friends be griev'd—
Among which number, Cassius, be you one—
Nor construe any further my neglect　　　50
Than that poor Brutus with himself at war
Forgets the shows of love to other men.

*Cassius*

Then, Brutus, I have much mistook your passion;
By means whereof this breast of mine hath buried
Thoughts of great value, worthy cogitations.　　55
Tell me, good Brutus, can you see your face?

*Brutus*

No, Cassius; for the eye sees not itself
But by reflection, by some other things.

*Cassius*

'Tis just:

67 **had his eyes**   could see clearly.

76 **jealous on**   suspicious of.
77–78 **did use/To stale**   was accustomed to cheapen by repeated use.

81 **scandal**   talk against.
82–83 **in banqueting/To all the rout**   in entertaining everyone
indiscriminately.

And it is very much lamented, Brutus,                    60
That you have no such mirrors as will turn
Your hidden worthiness into your eye,
That you might see your shadow. I have heard
Where many of the best respect in Rome,
Except immortal Cæsar, speaking of Brutus,               65
And groaning underneath this age's yoke,
Have wish'd that noble Brutus had his eyes.

*Brutus*

Into what dangers would you lead me, Cassius,
That you would have me seek into myself
For that which is not in me?                              70

*Cassius*

Therefore, good Brutus, be prepar'd to hear:
And since you know you cannot see yourself
So well as by reflection, I your glass
Will modestly discover to yourself
That of yourself which you yet know not of.              75
And be not jealous on me, gentle Brutus:
Were I a common laugher, or did use
To stale with ordinary oaths my love
To every new protester; if you know
That I do fawn on men and hug them hard,                 80
And after scandal them; or if you know
That I profess myself in banqueting
To all the rout, then hold me dangerous.
                          [*Flourish and shout.*

*Brutus*

What means this shouting? I do fear, the people
Choose Cæsar for their king.                             85

*Cassius*

                          Aye, do you fear it?
Then must I think you would not have it so.

*Brutus*

I would not, Cassius, yet I love him well.
But wherefore do you hold me here so long?

91 **aught**   anything.

93 **both**   some critics believe this should read "death," as suggested in the last two lines of Brutus's speech.

97 **favor**   appearance.

111 **accoutred**   fully equipped, probably in armor.

118 **Æneas**   according to legend, Æneas, the original founder of Rome, escaped from the burning city of Troy carrying his old father Anchises on his back and leading his wife and son Ascanius. Julius Cæsar claimed descent from this boy.

What is it that you would impart to me?                    90
If it be aught toward the general good,
Set honor in one eye and death i' th' other,
And I will look on both indifferently:
For let the gods so speed me as I love
The name of honor more than I fear death.                  95

*Cassius*

I know that virtue to be in you, Brutus,
As well as I do know your outward favor.
Well, honor is the subject of my story.
I cannot tell what you and other men
Think of this life, but, for my single self,               100
I had as lief not be as live to be
In awe of such a thing as I myself.
I was born free as Cæsar; so were you:
We both have fed as well, and we can both
Endure the winter's cold as well as he:                    105
For once, upon a raw and gusty day,
The troubled Tiber chafing with her shores,
Cæsar said to me, "Dar'st thou, Cassius, now
Leap in with me into this angry flood,
And swim to yonder point?" Upon the word,                  110
Accoutred as I was, I plunged in
And bade him follow: so indeed he did.
The torrent roar'd, and we did buffet it
With lusty sinews, throwing it aside
And stemming it with hearts of controversy;                115
But ere we could arrive the point propos'd,
Cæsar cried "Help me, Cassius, or I sink!"
I, as Æneas our great ancestor
Did from the flames of Troy upon his shoulder
The old Anchises bear, so from the waves of Tiber          120
Did I the tired Cæsar: and this man
Is now become a god, and Cassius is
A wretched creature, and must bend his body
If Cæsar carelessly but nod on him.

128 **coward lips**  this is oddly expressed but the allusion is apparently to the coward who drops his country's "colors," or flag, and deserts.

136 **get the start of**  outdistance.
137 **bear the palm**  receive the ultimate prize.

142 **Colossus**  the legendary bronze statue of Apollo at Rhodes; one of the seven wonders of the ancient world.

He had a fever when he was in Spain,                    125
And when the fit was on him, I did mark
How he did shake: 'tis true, this god did shake;
His coward lips did from their color fly,
And that same eye whose bend doth awe the world
Did lose his luster: I did hear him groan:             130
Aye, and that tongue of his that bade the Romans
Mark him and write his speeches in their books,
Alas, it cried, "Give me some drink, Titinius,"
As a sick girl. Ye gods! it doth amaze me
A man of such a feeble temper should                   135
So get the start of the majestic world
And bear the palm alone.

                              [*Shout. Flourish.*

*Brutus*

Another general shout!
I do believe that these applauses are
For some new honors that are heap'd on Cæsar.          140

*Cassius*

Why, man, he doth bestride the narrow world
Like a Colossus, and we petty men
Walk under his huge legs and peep about
To find ourselves dishonorable graves.
Men at some time are masters of their fates:           145
The fault, dear Brutus, is not in our stars,
But in ourselves, that we are underlings.
Brutus and Cæsar: what should be in that Cæsar?
Why should that name be sounded more than yours?
Write them together, yours is as fair a name;          150
Sound them, it doth become the mouth as well;
Weigh them, it is as heavy; conjure with 'em,
Brutus will start a spirit as soon as Cæsar.
Now, in the names of all the gods at once,
Upon what meat doth this our Cæsar feed,               155
That he is grown so great? Age, thou art sham'd!
Rome, thou hast lost the breed of noble bloods!

165 **a Brutus once** Lucius Junius Brutus, an ancestor, who according to legend drove out the tyrannical Tarquin, the last of the ancient Roman kings.
**brook'd** opposed.

168 **jealous** again, suspicious or unwilling.

176 **meet** appropriate.

180 **under these hard conditions** under such hard conditions.

When went there by an age, since the great flood,
But it was fam'd with more than with one man?
When could they say till now that talk'd of Rome          160
That her wide walls encompass'd but one man?
Now is it Rome indeed, and room enough,
When there is in it but one only man.
O, you and I have heard our fathers say
There was a Brutus once that would have brook'd          165
The eternal devil to keep his state in Rome
As easily as a king.

*Brutus*

That you do love me, I am nothing jealous;
What you would work me to, I have some aim:
How I have thought of this and of these times,          170
I shall recount hereafter; for this present,
I would not, so with love I might entreat you,
Be any further mov'd. What you have said
I will consider; what you have to say
I will with patience hear, and find a time          175
Both meet to hear and answer such high things.
Till then, my noble friend, chew upon this:
Brutus had rather be a villager
Than to repute himself a son of Rome
Under these hard conditions as this time          180
Is like to lay upon us.

*Cassius*

I am glad that my weak words
Have struck but thus much show of fire from Brutus.

*Brutus*

The games are done, and Cæsar is returning.

*Cassius*

As they pass by, pluck Casca by the sleeve;          185
And he will, after his sour fashion, tell you
What hath proceeded worthy note today.

   *Reenter Cæsar and his Train.*

190 **chidden train**   scolded group of followers.

200 **yond**   yonder, that.

204 **would**   I wish.

Brutus

    I will do so: but, look you, Cassius,
    The angry spot doth glow on Cæsar's brow,
    And all the rest look like a chidden train:          190
    Calpurnia's cheek is pale, and Cicero
    Looks with such ferret and such fiery eyes
    As we have seen him in the Capitol,
    Being cross'd in conference by some senators.

Cassius

    Casca will tell us what the matter is.          195

Cæsar

    Antonius!

Antony

    Cæsar?

Cæsar

    Let me have men about me that are fat,
    Sleek-headed men, and such as sleep o' nights:
    Yond Cassius has a lean and hungry look;          200
    He thinks too much: such men are dangerous.

Antony

    Fear him not, Cæsar; he's not dangerous;
    He is a noble Roman, and well given.

Cæsar

    Would he were fatter! but I fear him not:
    Yet if my name were liable to fear,          205
    I do not know the man I should avoid
    So soon as that spare Cassius. He reads much;
    He is a great observer, and he looks
    Quite through the deeds of men: he loves no plays,
    As thou dost, Antony; he hears no music:          210
    Seldom he smiles, and smiles in such a sort
    As if he mock'd himself, and scorn'd his spirit
    That could be mov'd to smile at any thing.
    Such men as he be never at heart's ease
    Whiles they behold a greater than themselves,          215
    And therefore are they very dangerous.

219 **come on**  come around to.

227 **put it by**  refused it.

234 **marry**  an Elizabethan exclamation of surprise, probably a variant of Mary, the Virgin.

I rather tell thee what is to be fear'd
Than what I fear; for always I am Cæsar.
Come on my right hand, for this ear is deaf,
And tell me truly what thou think'st of him.          220
     [*Sennet. Exeunt Cæsar and all his train but Casca.*

*Casca*
     You pull'd me by the cloak; would you speak with
          me?

*Brutus*
     Aye, Casca; tell us what hath chanc'd today,
     That Cæsar looks so sad.

*Casca*
     Why, you were with him, were you not?

*Brutus*
     I should not then ask Casca what had chanc'd.          225

*Casca*
     Why, there was a crown offered him: and being offered
     him, he put it by with the back of his hand, thus: and
     then the people fell a-shouting.

*Brutus*
     What was the second noise for?

*Casca*
     Why, for that too.          230

*Cassius*
     They shouted thrice: what was the last cry for?

*Casca*
     Why, for that too.

*Brutus*
     Was the crown offered him thrice?

*Casca*
     Aye, marry, was't, and he put it by thrice, every time
     gentler than other; and at every putting by mine hon-          235
     est neighbors shouted.

*Cassius*
     Who offered him the crown?

**244 fain** willingly.

**259 the falling sickness** epilepsy.

*Casca*
   Why, Antony.

*Brutus*
   Tell us the manner of it, gentle Casca.

*Casca*
   I can as well be hanged as tell the manner of it: it was          240
   mere foolery; I did not mark it. I saw Mark Antony
   offer him a crown: yet 'twas not a crown neither, 'twas
   one of these coronets: and, as I told you, he put it by
   once: but for all that, to my thinking, he would fain
   have had it. Then he offered it to him again; then he          245
   put it by again: but, to my thinking, he was very loath
   to lay his fingers off it. And then he offered it the third
   time; he put it the third time by: and still as he
   refused it, the rabblement hooted and clapped their
   chopped hands and threw up their sweaty night-caps          50
   and uttered such a deal of stinking breath because
   Cæsar refused the crown, that it had almost choked
   Cæsar; for he swounded and fell down at it: and for
   mine own part, I durst not laugh, for fear of opening
   my lips and receiving the bad air.          255

*Cassius*
   But, soft, I pray you: what, did Cæsar swound?

*Casca*
   He fell down in the market-place and foamed at mouth
   and was speechless.

*Brutus*
   'Tis very like: he hath the falling-sickness.

*Cassius*
   No, Cæsar hath it not: but you, and I,          260
   And honest Casca, we have the falling-sickness.

*Casca*
   I know not what you mean by that, but I am sure
   Cæsar fell down. If the tag-rag people did not clap him
   and hiss him according as he pleased and displeased

270 **plucked me ope his doublet**   opened his doublet or shirt.

291 **put to silence**   probably, relieved of their positions. Some interpret it as put to death.

them, as they used to do the players in the theater,  265
I am no true man.

Brutus

What said he when he came unto himself?

Casca

Marry, before he fell down, when he perceived the
common herd was glad he refused the crown, he
plucked me ope his doublet and offered them his  27(
throat to cut. An I had been a man of any occupation,
if I would not have taken him at a word, I would I
might go to hell among the rogues. And so he fell.
When he came to himself again, he said, if he had
done or said anything amiss, he desired their worships  275
to think it was his infirmity. Three or four wenches,
where I stood, cried "Alas, good soul!" and forgave
him with all their hearts: but there's no heed to be
taken of them; if Cæsar had stabbed their mothers,
they would have done no less.  280

Brutus

And after that, he came, thus sad, away?

Casca

Aye.

Cassius

Did Cicero say any thing?

Casca

Aye, he spoke Greek.

Cassius

To what effect?  285

Casca

Nay, an I tell you that, I'll ne'er look you i' the face
again: but those that understood him smiled at one
another and shook their heads; but for mine own part,
it was Greek to me. I could tell you more news too:
Marullus and Flavius, for pulling scarfs off Cæsar's  290
images, are put to silence. Fare you well. There was
more foolery yet, if I could remember it.

301 **quick metal**   quick-witted.

304 **tardy form**   pose of stupidity or obtuseness.

315 **from that**   from the condition to which it ıs ordinarily disposed.

*Cassius*

Will you sup with me tonight, Casca?

*Casca*

No, I am promis'd forth.

*Cassius*

Will you dine with me tomorrow?                               295

*Casca*

Aye, if I be alive, and your mind hold, and your dinner
worth the eating.

*Cassius*

Good; I will expect you.

*Casca*

Do so: farewell, both.

                                            [*Exit.*

*Brutus*

What a blunt fellow is this grown to be!                      300
He was quick metal when he went to school.

*Cassius*

So is he now in execution
Of any bold or noble enterprise,
However he puts on this tardy form.
This rudeness is a sauce to his good wit,                     305
Which gives men stomach to digest his words
With better appetite.

*Brutus*

And so it is. For this time I will leave you:
Tomorrow, if you please to speak with me,
I will come home to you, or, if you will,                     310
Come home to me and I will wait for you.

*Cassius*

I will do so: till then, think of the world.

                                    [*Exit Brutus.*

Well, Brutus, thou art noble; yet, I see,
Thy honorable metal may be wrought
From that it is dispos'd: therefore, it is meet               315

319–320 Cassius here shows his utter cynicism and opportunism by mocking Brutus for having been influenced so easily. Cassius implies that Brutus, being in favor with Cæsar, is a fool for listening to him, that Cassius himself would not have done so if their positions were reversed.

10 **dropping fire**   meteors.

That noble minds keep ever with their likes;
For who so firm that cannot be seduc'd?
Cæsar doth bear me hard; but he loves Brutus:
If I were Brutus now and he were Cassius,
He should not humor me. I will this night,          320
In several hands, in at his windows throw,
As if they came from several citizens,
Writings, all tending to the great opinion
That Rome holds of his name, wherein obscurely
Cæsar's ambition shall be glanced at:          325
And after this let Cæsar seat him sure;
For we will shake him, or worse days endure.

[*Exit.*

## Scene 3. *A street*

*Thunder and Lightning. Enter, from opposite sides, Casca, with his sword drawn, and Cicero.*

*Cicero*

Good even, Casca: brought you Cæsar home?
Why are you breathless? and why stare you so?

*Casca*

Are not you moved, when all the sway of earth
Shakes like a thing unfirm? O Cicero,
I have seen tempests, when the scolding winds          5
Have riv'd the knotty oaks, and I have seen
Th' ambitious ocean swell and rage and foam,
To be exalted with the threat'ning clouds;
But never till tonight, never till now,
Did I go through a tempest dropping fire.          10
Either there is a civil strife in heaven,
Or else the world too saucy with the gods
Incenses them to send destruction.

18 **sensible**   aware.

21 **glaz'd**   glared.

26 **bird of night**   the owl.

29 **conjointly meet**   occur at the same time.

32 **climate**   country, region.

35 **clean from**   completely different from.

*Cicero*

Why, saw you any thing more wonderful?

*Casca*

A common slave—you know him well by sight—          15
Held up his left hand, which did flame and burn
Like twenty torches join'd, and yet his hand
Not sensible of fire remain'd unscorch'd.
Besides—I ha' not since put up my sword—
Against the Capitol I met a lion,                    20
Who glaz'd upon me and went surly by
Without annoying me: and there were drawn
Upon a heap a hundred ghastly women
Transformed with their fear, who swore they saw
Men all in fire walk up and down the streets.        25
And yesterday the bird of night did sit
Even at noon-day upon the market-place,
Hooting and shrieking. When these prodigies
Do so conjointly meet, let not men say
"These are their reasons: they are natural:"          30
For, I believe, they are portentous things
Unto the climate that they point upon.

*Cicero*

Indeed, it is a strange-disposed time:
But men may construe things after their fashion,
Clean from the purpose of the things themselves.     35
Comes Cæsar to the Capitol tomorrow?

*Casca*

He doth; for he did bid Antonius
Send word to you he would be there tomorrow.

*Cicero*

Good night then, Casca: this disturbed sky
Is not to walk in.                                    40

*Casca*

                    Farewell, Cicero.

                              [*Exit Cicero.*

    *Enter Cassius.*

51 **unbraced**   with doublet unbuttoned or unlaced.

59 **astonish**   strike with awe.

61 **want**   lack.

67 **from quality and kind**   deviate from their usual condition
and nature.

*Cassius*
　Who's there?
*Casca*
　　　　　A Roman.
*Cassius*
　　　　　　　　Casca, by your voice.
*Casca*
　Your ear is good. Cassius, what night is this!　　　45
*Cassius*
　A very pleasing night to honest men.
*Casca*
　Who ever knew the heavens menace so?
*Cassius*
　Those that have known the earth so full of faults.
　For my part, I have walk'd about the streets,
　Submitting me unto the perilous night,　　　　　50
　And thus unbraced, Casca, as you see,
　Have bar'd my bosom to the thunder-stone;
　And when the cross blue lightning seem'd to open
　The breast of heaven, I did present myself
　Even in the aim and very flash of it.　　　　　55
*Casca*
　But wherefore did you so much tempt the heavens?
　It is the part of men to fear and tremble
　When the most mighty gods by tokens send
　Such dreadful heralds to astonish us.
*Cassius*
　You are dull, Casca, and those sparks of life　　60
　That should be in a Roman you do want,
　Or else you use not. You look pale and gaze
　And put on fear and cast yourself in wonder,
　To see the strange impatience of the heavens:
　But if you would consider the true cause　　　　65
　Why all these fires, why all these gliding ghosts,
　Why birds and beasts from quality and kind,

74 **monstrous** abnormal.

84 **thews** muscles.
85 **woe the while** alas! what a time!

87 **yoke and sufferance** endurance of suppression.

Why old men fool and children calculate,
Why all these things change from their ordinance,
Their natures and preformed faculties,                      70
To monstrous quality, why, you shall find
That heaven hath infus'd them with these spirits
To make them instruments of fear and warning
Unto some monstrous state.
Now could I, Casca, name to thee a man                       75
Most like this dreadful night,
That thunders, lightens, opens graves, and roars
As doth the lion in the Capitol,
A man no mightier than thyself or me
In personal action, yet prodigious grown                     80
And fearful, as these strange eruptions are.

*Casca*
'Tis Cæsar that you mean; is it not, Cassius?

*Cassius*
Let it be who it is: for Romans now
Have thews and limbs like to their ancestors;
But, woe the while! our fathers' minds are dead,             85
And we are govern'd with our mothers' spirits;
Our yoke and sufferance show us womanish.

*Casca*
Indeed they say the senators tomorrow
Mean to establish Cæsar as a king;
And he shall wear his crown by sea and land,                 90
In every place save here in Italy.

*Cassius*
I know where I will wear this dagger then:
Cassius from bondage will deliver Cassius.
Therein, ye gods, you make the weak most strong;
Therein, ye gods, you tyrants do defeat:                     95
Nor stony tower, nor walls of beaten brass,
Nor airless dungeon, nor strong links of iron,
Can be retentive to the strength of spirit;
But life, being weary of these worldly bars,

113 **offal**   refuse, rubbish.

121 **fleering**   sneering, laughing coarsely.
122 **Be factious**   be a part of the faction.

Never lacks power to dismiss itself.     100
If I know this, know all the world besides,
That part of tyranny that I do bear
I can shake off at pleasure.

*[Thunder still.*

Casca

So can I:
So every bondman in his own hand bears     105
The power to cancel his captivity.

Cassius

And why should Cæsar be a tyrant then?
Poor man! I know he would not be a wolf
But that he sees the Romans are but sheep:
He were no lion, were not Romans hinds.     110
Those that with haste will make a mighty fire
Begin it with weak straws: what trash is Rome,
What rubbish and what offal, when it serves
For the base matter to illuminate
So vile a thing as Cæsar! But, O grief,     115
Where hast thou led me? I perhaps speak this
Before a willing bondman; then I know
My answer must be made. But I am arm'd,
And dangers are to me indifferent.

Casca

You speak to Casca, and to such a man     120
That is no fleering tell-tale. Hold, my hand:
Be factious for redress of all these griefs,
And I will set this foot of mine as far
As who goes farthest.

Cassius

There's a bargain made.     125
Now know you, Casca, I have mov'd already
Some certain of the noblest-minded Romans
To undergo with me an enterprise
Of honorable-dangerous consequence;
And I do know, by this they stay for me     130

131 **Pompey's porch**   the portico of Pompey's theater where, according to Plutarch, Cæsar was assassinated. Shakespeare, you will note, has the assassination occur in the Senate House, but still refers to Pompey's statue at whose feet Cæsar fell, according to tradition.

133 **complexion of the element**   nature of the weather.

149 **praetor's chair**   Brutus was praetor (magistrate) of Rome.

151 **set this up with wax**   affix this document with wax to the statue of Brutus's ancestor.

In Pompey's porch: for now, this fearful night,
There is no stir or walking in the streets,
And the complexion of the element
In favor's like the work we have in hand,
Most bloody, fiery, and most terrible.                    135

*Enter Cinna.*

**Casca**
Stand close awhile, for here comes one in haste.
**Cassius**
'Tis Cinna; I do know him by his gait;
He is a friend. Cinna, where haste you so?
**Cinna**
To find out you. Who's that? Metellus Cimber?
**Cassius**
No, it is Casca; one incorporate                          140
To our attempts. Am I not stay'd for, Cinna?
**Cinna**
I am glad on 't. What a fearful night is this!
There's two or three of us have seen strange sights.
**Cassius**
Am I not stay'd for? tell me.
**Cinna**
                              Yes, you are.               145
O Cassius, if you could
But win the noble Brutus to our party—
**Cassius**
Be you content: good Cinna, take this paper,
And look you lay it in the prætor's chair,
Where Brutus may but find it, and throw this              150
In at his window; set this up with wax
Upon old Brutus' statue: all this done,
Repair to Pompey's porch, where you shall find us.
Is Decius Brutus and Trebonius there?

**Cinna**
All but Metellus Cimber; and he's gone                    155

156 **hie**  hasten.

158 **repair**  go.

159 **ere**  before.

168 **conceited**  thought out, expressed.

    To seek you at your house. Well, I will hie,
    And so bestow these papers as you bade me.
*Cassius*
    That done, repair to Pompey's theater.

                                      [*Exit Cinna.*

    Come, Casca, you and I will yet ere day
    See Brutus at his house: three parts of him          160
    Is ours already, and the man entire
    Upon the next encounter yields him ours.
*Casca*
    O, he sits high in all the people's hearts;
    And that which would appear offense in us
    His countenance, like richest alchemy,               165
    Will change to virtue and to worthiness.
*Cassius*
    Him and his worth and our great need of him
    You have right well conceited. Let us go,
    For it is after midnight, and ere day
    We will awake him and be sure of him.                170

                                      [*Exeunt.*


# ACT II


*Scene 1. Rome. Brutus's orchard*

*Enter Brutus.*


*Brutus*
    What, Lucius, ho!
    I cannot, by the progress of the stars,
    Give guess how near to day. Lucius, I say!
    I would it were my fault to sleep so soundly.
    When, Lucius, when? awake, I say! what, Lucius!       5

11 **spurn**   oppose.
12 **for the general**   for the general welfare, the country.

15 **craves**   requires.

19 **remorse**   pity.
20 **affections sway'd**   feelings weighed.

33 **as his kind**   like his kind (the serpent).

*Enter Lucius.*

**Lucius**
  Call'd you, my lord?
**Brutus**
  Get me a taper in my study, Lucius:
  When it is lighted, come and call me here.
**Lucius**
  I will, my lord.

                          [*Exit.*

**Brutus**
  It must be by his death: and, for my part,                    10
  I know no personal cause to spurn at him,
  But for the general. He would be crown'd:
  How that might change his nature, there's the
      question:
  It is the bright day that brings forth the adder;
  And that craves wary walking. Crown him?—that—       15
  And then, I grant, we put a sting in him,
  That at his will he may do danger with.
  Th' abuse of greatness is when it disjoins
  Remorse from power: and, to speak truth of Cæsar,
  I have not known when his affections sway'd            20
  More than his reason. But 'tis a common proof,
  That lowliness is young ambition's ladder,
  Whereto the climber-upward turns his face;
  But when he once attains the upmost round,
  He then unto the ladder turns his back,                25
  Looks in the clouds, scorning the base degrees
  By which he did ascend: so Cæsar may;
  Then, lest he may, prevent. And, since the quarrel
  Will bear no color for the thing he is,
  Fashion it thus; that what he is, augmented,            30
  Would run to these and these extremities:
  And therefore think him as a serpent's egg
  Which hatch'd would as his kind grow mischievous,
  And kill him in the shell.

35 **closet**   study, private chamber.

44 **exhalations**   meteors.

51 **piece it out**   fill in what has been left out.

*Reenter Lucius.*

Lucius

The taper burneth in your closet, sir.                    35
Searching the window for a flint I found
This paper thus seal'd up, and I am sure
It did not lie there when I went to bed.
                              [*Gives him the letter.*

Brutus

Get you to bed again; it is not day.
Is not tomorrow, boy, the ides of March?                  40

Lucius

I know not, sir.

Brutus

Look in the calendar and bring me word.

Lucius

I will, sir.
                                              [*Exit.*

Brutus

The exhalations whizzing in the air
Give so much light that I may read by them.              45
                              [*Opens the letter and reads.*
"Brutus, thou sleep'st: awake and see thyself.
Shall Rome, &c. Speak, strike, redress.
Brutus, thou sleep'st: awake."
Such instigations have been often dropp'd
Where I have took them up.                                50
"Shall Rome, &c." Thus must I piece it out:
Shall Rome stand under one man's awe? What, Rome?
My ancestors did from the streets of Rome
The Tarquin drive, when he was call'd a king.
"Speak, strike, redress." Am I entreated                 55
To speak and strike? O Rome, I make thee promise,
If the redress will follow, thou receivest
Thy full petition at the hand of Brutus!

*Reenter Lucius.*

66 **Genius**   inner self or guardian spirit.
   **mortal instruments**   impulses to deadly actions.

70 **your brother**   Cassius was married to Junia, Brutus's sister.

73 **moe**   more.

78 **any mark of favor**   any recognizable physical characteristic.

Lucius
>  Sir, March is wasted fifteen days.

> [*Knocking within.*

Brutus
>  'Tis good. Go to the gate; somebody knocks.    60

> [*Exit Lucius.*

>  Since Cassius first did whet me against Cæsar
>  I have not slept.
>  Between the acting of a dreadful thing
>  And the first motion, all the interim is
>  Like a phantasma or a hideous dream:    65
>  The Genius and the mortal instruments
>  Are then in council, and the state of man,
>  Like to a little kingdom, suffers then
>  The nature of an insurrection.

> *Reenter Lucius.*

Lucius
>  Sir, 'tis your brother Cassius at the door,    70
>  Who doth desire to see you.

Brutus
>                              Is he alone?

Lucius
>  No, sir, there are moe with him.

Brutus
>                              Do you know them?

Lucius
>  No, sir: their hats are pluck'd about their ears,    75
>  And half their faces buried in their cloaks,
>  That by no means I may discover them
>  By any mark of favor.

Brutus
>                  Let 'em enter.

> [*Exit Lucius.*

>  They are the faction. O conspiracy,    80
>  Sham'st thou to show thy dang'rous brow by night,
>  When evils are most free? O, then, by day

86 **path** (used as a verb) continue in the usual way.

87 **Erebus** a place of darkness through which, according to Greek legend, the dead passed on their way to Hell or Hades.

88 **prevention** detection.

89 **too bold upon your rest** have gotten you up too early.

103 **watchful cares** troubles that prevent sleep.

Where wilt thou find a cavern dark enough
To mask thy monstrous visage? Seek none, conspiracy;
Hide it in smiles and affability:                                    85
For if thou path, thy native semblance on,
Not Erebus itself were dim enough
To hide thee from prevention.

*Enter the conspirators, Cassius, Casca, Decius,*
*Cinna, Metellus Cimber, and Trebonius.*

*Cassius*

I think we are too bold upon your rest:
Good morrow, Brutus; do we trouble you?                    90

*Brutus*

I have been up this hour, awake all night.
Know I these men that come along with you?

*Cassius*

Yes, every man of them; and no man here
But honors you; and everyone doth wish
You had but that opinion of yourself                            95
Which every noble Roman bears of you.
This is Trebonius.

*Brutus*

                          He is welcome hither.

*Cassius*

This, Decius Brutus.

*Brutus*

                          He is welcome too.                        100

*Cassius*

This, Casca; this, Cinna; and this, Metellus Cimber.

*Brutus*

They are all welcome.
What watchful cares do interpose themselves
Betwixt your eyes and night?

*Cassius*

Shall I entreat a word?                                              105

                          [*They whisper.*

109 **fret**   make a design like a fretwork.

112 **a great way growing on**   inclining a great deal toward.
113 **weighing**   considering, in view of.

119 **the face of men**   possibly public opinion; or a reference
   to the dejected looks of men in these troubled times.
121 **betimes**   before it is too late.

131 **palter**   haggle, deal crookedly or dishonestly.

134 **men cautelous**   overcautious men.

*Decius*
  Here lies the east: doth not the day break here?
*Casca*
  No.
*Cinna*
  O, pardon, sir, it doth, and yon gray lines
  That fret the clouds are messengers of day.
*Casca*
  You shall confess that you are both deceiv'd.          110
  Here, as I point my sword, the sun arises;
  Which is a great way growing on the south,
  Weighing the youthful season of the year.
  Some two months hence up higher toward the north
  He first presents his fire, and the high east          115
  Stands as the Capitol, directly here.

*Brutus*
  Give me your hands all over, one by one.

*Cassius*
  And let us swear our resolution.

*Brutus*
  No, not an oath: if not the face of men,
  The sufferance of our souls, the time's abuse—         120
  If these be motives weak, break off betimes,
  And every man hence to his idle bed;
  So let high-sighted tyranny range on
  Till each man drop by lottery. But if these,
  As I am sure they do, bear fire enough                 125
  To kindle cowards and to steel with valor
  The melting spirits of women, then, countrymen,
  What need we any spur but our own cause
  To prick us to redress? what other bond
  Than secret Romans that have spoke the word,           130
  And will not palter? and what other oath
  Than honesty to honesty engaged
  That this shall be or we will fall for it?
  Swear priests and cowards and men cautelous,

135 **carrions**   rottenness or rotten things.

140 **or our cause or our performance**   either our cause or our
performance.

143 **a several bastardy**   many falsities or illegitimacies.

146 **sound**   measure, find out where he stands.

154 **whit**   bit.

156 **break with him**   take him into our confidence.

    Old feeble carrions and such suffering souls          135
    That welcome wrongs; unto bad causes swear
    Such creatures as men doubt: but do not stain
    The even virtue of our enterprise,
    Nor th' insuppressive mettle of our spirits,
    To think that or our cause or our performance          140
    Did need an oath; when every drop of blood
    That every Roman bears, and nobly bears,
    Is guilty of a several bastardy
    If he do break the smallest particle
    Of any promise that hath pass'd from him.          145

*Cassius*
    But what of Cicero? shall we sound him?
    I think he will stand very strong with us.

*Casca*
    Let us not leave him out.

*Cinna*
                  No, by no means.

*Metellus*
    O, let us have him, for his silver hairs          150
    Will purchase us a good opinion,
    And buy men's voices to commend our deeds:
    It shall be said his judgment ruled our hands;
    Our youths and wildness shall no whit appear,
    But all be buried in his gravity.          155

*Brutus*
    O, name him not: let us not break with him,
    For he will never follow any thing
    That other men begin.

*Cassius*
                  Then leave him out.

*Casca*
    Indeed he is not fit.          160

*Decius*
    Shall no man else be touch'd but only Cæsar?

171 **like wrath in death and envy afterwards** like killing in anger and then mutilating the body from malice.

176 **come by** arrive at, find.

185 **envious** malicious.

*Cassius*
    Decius, well urg'd: I think it is not meet
    Mark Antony, so well beloved of Cæsar,
    Should outlive Cæsar: we shall find of him
    A shrewd contriver; and you know his means,    165
    If he improve them, may well stretch so far
    As to annoy us all: which to prevent,
    Let Antony and Cæsar fall together.

*Brutus*
    Our course will seem too bloody, Caius Cassius,
    To cut the head off and then hack the limbs,    170
    Like wrath in death and envy afterwards;
    For Antony is but a limb of Cæsar:
    Let us be sacrificers, but not butchers, Caius.
    We all stand up against the spirit of Cæsar,
    And in the spirit of men there is no blood:    175
    O, that we then could come by Cæsar's spirit,
    And not dismember Cæsar? But, alas,
    Cæsar must bleed for it! And, gentle friends,
    Let's kill him boldly, but not wrathfully;
    Let's carve him as a dish fit for the gods,    180
    Not hew him as a carcass fit for hounds:
    And let our hearts, as subtle masters do,
    Stir up their servants to an act of rage
    And after seem to chide 'em. This shall make
    Our purpose necessary and not envious:    185
    Which so appearing to the common eyes,
    We shall be call'd purgers, not murderers.
    And for Mark Antony, think not of him;
    For he can do no more than Cæsar's arm
    When Cæsar's head is off.    190

*Cassius*
                   Yet I fear him,
    For in the ingrafted love he bears to Cæsar—

*Brutus*
    Alas, good Cassius, do not think of him:
    If he love Cæsar, all that he can do

210 **augurers** Roman officials charged with observing and interpreting omens for guidance in public affairs.

213–216 Various myths connected with mythical or symbolical beasts are here mentioned. The unicorn, a mythical beast with one horn in the middle of its forehead, was supposed to be caught by tricking it to run into a tree; bears could be fooled by camouflaging pits; etc.

Is to himself, take thought and die for Cæsar:          195
And that were much he should, for he is given
To sports, to wildness and much company.

*Trebonius*

There is no fear in him; let him not die;
For he will live and laugh at this hereafter.

                      [*Clock strikes.*

*Brutus*

Peace! count the clock.                                  200

*Cassius*

               The clock hath stricken three.

*Trebonius*

'Tis time to part.

*Cassius*

             But it is doubtful yet
Whether Cæsar will come forth today or no;
For he is superstitious grown of late,                   205
Quite from the main opinion he held once
Of fantasy, of dreams and ceremonies:
It may be these apparent prodigies,
The unaccustom'd terror of this night
And the persuasion of his augurers,                      210
May hold him from the Capitol today.

*Decius*

Never fear that: if he be so resolved,
I can o'ersway him; for he loves to hear
That unicorns may be betray'd with trees
And bears with glasses, elephants with holes,            215
Lions with toils and men with flatterers:
But when I tell him he hates flatterers,
He says he does, being then most flattered.
Let me work;
For I can give his humor the true bent,                  220
And I will bring him to the Capitol.

*Cassius*

Nay, we will all of us be there to fetch him.

225 **bear Cæsar hard** oppose.

235 **put on** suggest.

Brutus

    By the eighth hour: is that the uttermost?

Cinna

    Be that the uttermost, and fail not then.

Metellus

    Caius Ligarius doth bear Cæsar hard,                        225

    Who rated him for speaking well of Pompey:

    I wonder none of you have thought of him.

Brutus

    Now, good Metellus, go along by him:

    He loves me well, and I have given him reasons;

    Send him but hither, and I'll fashion him.                  230

Cassius

    The morning comes upon 's: we'll leave you, Brutus:

    And, friends, disperse yourselves: but all remember

    What you have said and show yourselves true Romans.

Brutus

    Good gentlemen, look fresh and merrily;

    Let not our looks put on our purposes;                      235

    But bear it as our Roman actors do,

    With untired spirits and formal constancy:

    And so, good morrow to you every one.

                     [*Exeunt all but Brutus.*

    Boy! Lucius! Fast asleep! It is no matter;

    Enjoy the honey-heavy dew of slumber:                       240

    Thou hast no figures nor no fantasies,

    Which busy care draws in the brains of men;

    Therefore thou sleep'st so sound.

    *Enter Portia.*

Portia

                     Brutus, my lord!

Brutus

    Portia, what mean you? wherefore rise you now?              245

    It is not for your health thus to commit

    Your weak condition to the raw cold morning.

257 **wafture**  waving.

272 **physical**  healthful.

277 **rheumy**  damp.

Portia

    Nor for yours neither. You've ungently, Brutus,
    Stole from my bed: and yesternight at supper
    You suddenly arose and walk'd about,           250
    Musing and sighing, with your arms across;
    And when I ask'd you what the matter was,
    You star'd upon me with ungentle looks:
    I urg'd you further; then you scratch'd your head,
    And too impatiently stamp'd with your foot:     255
    Yet I insisted, yet you answer'd not,
    But with an angry wafture of your hand
    Gave sign for me to leave you: so I did,
    Fearing to strengthen that impatience
    Which seem'd too much enkindled, and withal   260
    Hoping it was but an effect of humor,
    Which sometime hath his hour with every man.
    It will not let you eat, nor talk, nor sleep,
    And, could it work so much upon your shape
    As it hath much prevail'd on your condition,    265
    I should not know you, Brutus. Dear my lord,
    Make me acquainted with your cause of grief.

Brutus

    I am not well in health, and that is all.

Portia

    Brutus is wise, and, were he not in health,
    He would embrace the means to come by it.    270

Brutus

    Why, so I do: good Portia, go to bed.

Portia

    Is Brutus sick, and is it physical
    To walk unbraced and suck up the humors
    Of the dank morning? What, is Brutus sick,
    And will he steal out of his wholesome bed,    275
    To dare the vile contagion of the night,
    And tempt the rheumy and unpurged air
    To add unto his sickness? No, my Brutus;

297 **suburbs**   outermost parts.

307 **Cato**   Cato the Younger, Portia's father, was a Roman
patriot who upheld the old, simple virtues. He supported
Pompey against Cæsar. When Pompey was defeated, rather
than submit to Cæsar, Cato committed suicide by running
on his sword.

You have some sick offense within your mind,
Which by the right and virtue of my place      280
I ought to know of: and, upon my knees,
I charm you, by my once commended beauty,
By all your vows of love and that great vow
Which did incorporate and make us one,
That you unfold to me, yourself, your half,      285
Why you are heavy, and what men tonight
Have had resort to you; for here have been
Some six or seven, who did hide their faces
Even from darkness.

*Brutus*

                    Kneel not, gentle Portia.      290

*Portia*

I should not need, if you were gentle Brutus.
Within the bond of marriage, tell me, Brutus,
Is it expected I should know no secrets
That appertain to you? Am I yourself
But, as it were, in sort or limitation,      295
To keep with you at meals, comfort your bed,
And talk to you sometimes? Dwell I but in the suburbs
Of your good pleasure? If it be no more,
Portia is Brutus' harlot, not his wife.

*Brutus*

You are my true and honorable wife,      300
As dear to me as are the ruddy drops
That visit my sad heart.

*Portia*

If this were true, then should I know this secret.
I grant I am a woman, but withal
A woman that Lord Brutus took to wife:      305
I grant I am a woman, but withal
A woman well reputed, Cato's daughter.
Think you I am no stronger than my sex,
Being so father'd and so husbanded?
Tell me your counsels, I will not disclose 'em:      310

312 **voluntary wound**   As a test of her ability to bear any peril or secret of her husband, Portia had given herself a painful wound in the thigh with a razor.

326 **vouchsafe**   grant, permit.

I have made strong proof of my constancy,
Giving myself a voluntary wound
Here in the thigh: can I bear that with patience
And not my husband's secrets?

Brutus

                       O ye gods,                    315
Render me worthy of this noble wife!
                      [Knocking within.
Hark, hark! one knocks: Portia, go in a while;
And by and by thy bosom shall partake
The secrets of my heart:
All my engagements I will construe to thee,                320
All the charactery of my sad brows.
Leave me with haste. [Exit Portia.] Lucius, who's that
   knocks?

    Reenter Lucius with Ligarius.

Lucius
Here is a sick man that would speak with you.

Brutus
Caius Ligarius, that Metellus spake of.
Boy, stand aside. Caius Ligarius! how?                    325

Ligarius
Vouchsafe good morrow from a feeble tongue.

Brutus
O, what a time have you chose out, brave Caius,
To wear a kerchief! Would you were not sick!

Ligarius
I am not sick, if Brutus have in hand
Any exploit worthy the name of honor.                     330

Brutus
Such an exploit have I in hand, Ligarius,
Had you a healthful ear to hear of it.

Ligarius
By all the gods that Romans bow before,
I here discard my sickness! Soul of Rome!

339 **yea**   yes.

345 **set on your foot**   carry on.

Stage directions **night-gown**   dressing gown.

Brave son, deriv'd from honorable loins!　　　335
Thou, like an exorcist, hast conjur'd up
My mortified spirit. Now bid me run,
And I will strive with things impossible,
Yea, get the better of them. What's to do?

Brutus

A piece of work that will make sick men whole.　　　340

Ligarius

But are not some whole that we must make sick?

Brutus

That must we also. What it is, my Caius,
I shall unfold to thee, as we are going
To whom it must be done.

Ligarius

　　　　　　　　Set on your foot,　　　345
And with a heart new-fir'd I follow you,
To do I know not what: but it sufficeth
That Brutus leads me on.

Brutus

　　　　　　　　Follow me then.

　　　　　　　　　　　　　[Exeunt.


Scene 2. Cæsar's house

Thunder and lightning. Enter Cæsar, in his night-
gown.

Cæsar

Nor heaven nor earth have been at peace tonight:
Thrice hath Calpurnia in her sleep cried out,
"Help, ho! they murder Cæsar!" Who's within?

Enter a Servant.

5 **present** immediate.

13 **stood on ceremonies** paid attention to omens.
14 **one within** one within the house (possibly a servant).

16 **watch** Shakespeare referred here to the officers of the watch who patrolled the streets at night in his own time.

20 **right form of war** exact manner of war.

25 **beyond all use** outside the usual, extraordinary.

*Servant*
    My lord?

*Cæsar*
    Go bid the priests do present sacrifice,                          5
    And bring me their opinions of success.

*Servant*
    I will, my lord.

                                                        [*Exit.*

        *Enter Calpurnia.*

*Calpurnia*
    What mean you, Cæsar? think you to walk forth?
    You shall not stir out of your house today.

*Cæsar*
    Cæsar shall forth: the things that threaten'd me     10
    Ne'er look'd but on my back; when they shall see
    The face of Cæsar, they are vanished.

*Calpurnia*
    Cæsar, I never stood on ceremonies,
    Yet now they fright me. There is one within,
    Besides the things that we have heard and seen,      15
    Recounts most horrid sights seen by the watch.
    A lioness hath whelped in the streets;
    And graves have yawn'd, and yielded up their dead;
    Fierce fiery warriors fight upon the clouds,
    In ranks and squadrons and right form of war,        20
    Which drizzled blood upon the Capitol;
    The noise of battle hurtled in the air,
    Horses did neigh and dying men did groan,
    And ghosts did shriek and squeal about the streets.
    O Cæsar! these things are beyond all use,            25
    And I do fear them.

*Cæsar*
                        What can be avoided
    Whose end is purpos'd by the mighty gods?
    Yet Cæsar shall go forth; for these predictions

32 Shakespeare may have taken the idea of the fiery heavens from a Roman writer, Suetonius, who reported that a blazing star appeared for seven days during the celebration, instituted by Augustus (Cæsar's nephew), to honor Julius Cæsar. The common people regarded this as an indication of Cæsar's entering the realm of the gods.

Are to the world in general as to Cæsar.                    30
**Calpurnia**
  When beggars die, there are no comets seen;
  The heavens themselves blaze forth the death of
      princes.
**Cæsar**
  Cowards die many times before their death;
  The valiant never taste of death but once.
  Of all the wonders that I yet have heard,                    35
  It seems to me most strange that men should fear;
  Seeing that death, a necessary end,
  Will come when it will come.

      *Reenter Servant.*

                              What say the augurers?
**Servant**
  They would not have you to stir forth today.                    40
  Plucking the entrails of an offering forth,
  They could not find a heart within the beast.
**Cæsar**
  The gods do this in shame of cowardice:
  Cæsar should be a beast without a heart
  If he should stay at home today for fear.                    45
  No, Cæsar shall not: danger knows full well
  That Cæsar is more dangerous than he:
  We are two lions litter'd in one day,
  And I the elder and more terrible:
  And Cæsar shall go forth.                    50
**Calpurnia**
                    Alas, my lord,
  Your wisdom is consum'd in confidence.
  Do not go forth today: call it my fear
  That keeps you in the house and not your own.
  We'll send Mark Antony to the senate-house,                    55
  And he shall say you are not well today:
  Let me, upon my knee, prevail in this.

59 **humor**   whim.

79 **stays**   keeps.
80 **statuë**   here pronounced as three syllables.

*Cæsar*

    Mark Antony shall say I am not well,
    And, for thy humor, I will stay at home.

    *Enter Decius.*

    Here's Decius Brutus, he shall tell them so.　　60

*Decius*

    Cæsar, all hail! good morrow, worthy Cæsar:
    I come to fetch you to the senate-house.

*Cæsar*

    And you are come in very happy time,
    To bear my greeting to the senators
    And tell them that I will not come today:　　65
    Cannot, is false, and that I dare not, falser:
    I will not come today: tell them so, Decius.

*Calpurnia*

    Say he is sick.

*Cæsar*

            Shall Cæsar send a lie?
    Have I in conquest stretch'd mine arm so far,　　70
    To be afeard to tell graybeards the truth?
    Decius, go tell them Cæsar will not come.

*Decius*

    Most mighty Cæsar, let me know some cause,
    Lest I be laugh'd at when I tell them so.

*Cæsar*

    The cause is in my will: I will not come;　　75
    That is enough to satisfy the senate.
    But, for your private satisfaction,
    Because I love you, I will let you know.
    Calpurnia here, my wife, stays me at home:
    She dreamt tonight she saw my statuë,　　80
    Which like a fountain with an hundred spouts
    Did run pure blood, and many lusty Romans
    Came smiling and did bathe their hands in it:
    And these does she apply for warnings and portents

93 **tinctures**   tints.
**cognizance**   a heraldic term referring to a badge worn by servants or followers of a noble house.

100 **were**   would be.
101 **apt**   likely.
**render'd**   given in return.

105 **Lo**   interjection meaning "look" or "behold."

107 **proceeding**   success, advancement.
108 **reason to my love is liable**   my affection for you out-weighs my reason or judgment of what is appropriate.

And evils imminent, and on her knee                      85
Hath begg'd that I will stay at home today.

*Decius*

This dream is all amiss interpreted;
It was a vision fair and fortunate:
Your statue spouting blood in many pipes,
In which so many smiling Romans bathed,                  90
Signifies that from you great Rome shall suck
Reviving blood, and that great men shall press
For tinctures, stains, relics and cognizance.
This by Calpurnia's dream is signified.

*Cæsar*

And this way have you well expounded it.                 95

*Decius*

I have, when you have heard what I can say:
And know it now: the senate have concluded
To give this day a crown to mighty Cæsar.
If you shall send them word you will not come,
Their minds may change. Besides, it were a mock         100
Apt to be render'd, for some one to say
"Break up the senate till another time,
When Cæsar's wife shall meet with better dreams."
If Cæsar hide himself, shall they not whisper
"Lo, Cæsar is afraid"?                                   105
Pardon me, Cæsar, for my dear dear love
To your proceeding bids me tell you this,
And reason to my love is liable.

*Cæsar*

How foolish do your fears seem now, Calpurnia!
I am ashamed I did yield to them.                        110
Give me my robe, for I will go.

*Enter Publius, Brutus, Ligarius, Metellus, Casca,
Trebonius, and Cinna*

And look where Publius is come to fetch me.

117 **enemy**   Ligarius had supported Pompey in the Civil War.
118 **ague**   fever and chills.

*Publius*
　Good morrow, Cæsar.
*Cæsar*
　　　　　　　　Welcome, Publius.
　What, Brutus, are you stirr'd so early too?          115
　Good morrow, Casca. Caius Ligarius,
　Cæsar was ne'er so much your enemy
　As that same ague which hath made you lean.
　What is 't o'clock?
*Brutus*
　　　　　　　　Cæsar, 'tis strucken eight.          120
*Cæsar*
　I thank you for your pains and courtesy.

　　*Enter Antony.*

　See! Antony, that revels long o' nights,
　Is notwithstanding up. Good morrow, Antony.
*Antony*
　So to most noble Cæsar.
*Cæsar*
　　　　　　　　Bid them prepare within:          125
　I am to blame to be thus waited for.
　Now, Cinna: now, Metellus: what, Trebonius!
　I have an hour's talk in store for you;
　Remember that you call on me today:
　Be near me, that I may remember you.          130
*Trebonius*
　Cæsar, I will. [*Aside*] And so near will I be,
　That your best friends shall wish I had been further.
*Cæsar*
　Good friends, go in and taste some wine with me;
　And we like friends will straightway go together.
*Brutus*
　[*Aside*]　That every like is not the same, O Cæsar,          135
　The heart of Brutus yearns to think upon!
　　　　　　　　　　　　　　[*Exeunt.*

**7 security gives way to conspiracy** inattention to danger attracts enemy plots.

**13 emulation** envy.

**15 Fates** the three goddesses who, according to Greek legend, controlled the destinies of men.

**1 prithee** pray thee, beg you.

## Scene 3. A street near the Capitol

*Enter Artemidorus, reading a paper.*

Artemidorus
   "Cæsar, beware of Brutus; take heed of Cassius; come
   not near Casca; have an eye to Cinna; trust not Trebonius; mark well Metellus Cimber: Decius Brutus
   loves thee not: thou hast wronged Caius Ligarius.
   There is but one mind in all these men, and it is          5
   bent against Cæsar. If thou beest not immortal, look
   about you: security gives way to conspiracy. The
   mighty gods defend thee!
                              Thy lover, Artemidorus."
   Here will I stand till Cæsar pass along,                  10
   And as a suitor will I give him this.
   My heart laments that virtue cannot live
   Out of the teeth of emulation.
   If thou read this, O Cæsar, thou mayst live:
   If not, the Fates with traitors do contrive.              15
                                        [*Exit.*

## Scene 4. Another part of the same street, before
## the house of Brutus

*Enter Portia and Lucius.*

Portia
   I prithee, boy, run to the senate-house;
   Stay not to answer me, but get thee gone.
   Why dost thou stay?

21 **rumor** loud noise.
   **fray** battle.

23 **sooth** truly.

Lucius

> To know my errand, madam.

Portia

> I would have had thee there, and here again,     5
> Ere I can tell thee what thou shouldst do there.
> O constancy, be strong upon my side!
> Set a huge mountain 'tween my heart and tongue!
> I have a man's mind, but a woman's might.
> How hard it is for women to keep counsel!     10
> Art thou here yet?

Lucius

> Madam, what should I do?
> Run to the Capitol, and nothing else?
> And so return to you, and nothing else?

Portia

> Yes, bring me word, boy, if thy lord look well,     15
> For he went sickly forth: and take good note
> What Cæsar doth, what suitors press to him.
> Hark, boy! what noise is that?

Lucius

> I hear none, madam.

Portia

> Prithee, listen well:     20
> I heard a bustling rumor like a fray,
> And the wind brings it from the Capitol.

Lucius

> Sooth, madam, I hear nothing.

*Enter the Soothsayer.*

Portia

> Come hither, fellow: Which way hast thou been?

Soothsayer

> At mine own house, good lady.     25

Portia

> What is 't o'clock?

41 **void**   empty.

43 **Aye me**   interjection similar to "Alas!"

49 **merry**   cheerful, rather than gay.

**Soothsayer**

>                About the ninth hour, lady.

**Portia**

> Is Cæsar yet gone to the Capitol?

**Soothsayer**

> Madam, not yet: I go to take my stand,
> To see him pass on to the Capitol.                              30

**Portia**

> Thou hast some suit to Cæsar, hast thou not?

**Soothsayer**

> That I have, lady: if it will please Cæsar
> To be so good to Cæsar as to hear me,
> I shall beseech him to befriend himself.

**Portia**

> Why, know'st thou any harm's intended towards him?    35

**Soothsayer**

> None that I know will be, much that I fear may
>       chance.
> Good morrow to you. Here the street is narrow:
> The throng that follows Cæsar at the heels,
> Of senators, of prætors, common suitors,
> Will crowd a feeble man almost to death:                        40
> I'll get me to a place more void and there
> Speak to great Cæsar as he comes along.
>                                              [*Exit.*

**Portia**

> I must go in. Aye me, how weak a thing
> The heart of woman is! O Brutus,
> The heavens speed thee in thine enterprise!                     45
> Sure, the boy heard me. Brutus hath a suit
> That Cæsar will not grant. O, I grow faint.
> Run, Lucius, and commend me to my lord;
> Say I am merry: come to me again,
> And bring me word what he doth say to thee.                     50
>                                    [*Exeunt severally.*

3 **schedule**   letter.

5 **suit**   request.

8 **last serv'd**   What concerns Cæsar personally must be attended to last of all.

# ACT III

*A crowd of people; among them Artemidorus and
the Soothsayer. Flourish. Enter Cæsar, Brutus, Cassius, Casca, Decius, Metellus, Trebonius, Cinna,
Antony, Lepidus, Popilius, Publius, and others.*

**Cæsar**
The ides of March are come.

**Soothsayer**
Aye, Cæsar; but not gone.

**Artemidorus**
Hail, Cæsar! read this schedule.

**Decius**
Trebonius doth desire you to o'er-read,
At your best leisure, this his humble suit.                    5

**Artemidorus**
O Cæsar, read mine first; for mine's a suit
That touches Cæsar nearer: read it, great Cæsar.

**Cæsar**
What touches us ourself shall be last serv'd.

**Artemidorus**
Delay not, Cæsar; read it instantly.

**Cæsar**
What, is the fellow mad?                                       10

**Publius**
                        Sirrah, give place.

**Cassius**
What, urge you your petitions in the street?
Come to the Capitol.

20 **makes to**  acts toward.

31 **prefer**  offer.

32 **address'd**  ready.

*Cæsar goes up to the Senate House, the rest
following.*

Popilius
I wish your enterprise today may thrive.
Cassius
What enterprise, Popilius?                                    15
Popilius
                         Fare you well.
                              [*Advances to Cæsar.*
Brutus
What said Popilius Lena?
Cassius
He wish'd today our enterprise might thrive.
I fear our purpose is discovered.
Brutus
Look, how he makes to Cæsar: mark him.                        20
Cassius
Casca, be sudden, for we fear prevention.
Brutus, what shall be done? If this be known,
Cassius or Cæsar never shall turn back,
For I will slay myself.
Brutus
                    Cassius, be constant:                     25
Popilius Lena speaks not of our purposes;
For, look, he smiles, and Cæsar doth not change.
Cassius
Trebonius knows his time; for, look you, Brutus,
He draws Mark Antony out of the way.
                    [*Exeunt Antony and Trebonius.*
Decius
Where is Metellus Cimber? Let him go,                         30
And presently prefer his suit to Cæsar.
Brutus
He is address'd: press near and second him.

36 **puissant**   powerful.

42 **pre-ordinance and first decree**   the orderly manner in which affairs are normally conducted.
43 **fond**   foolish.
44 **rebel blood**   impulses which work against reasoned decisions.

55 **repealing**   recall.

Cinna

Casca, you are the first that rears your hand.

Cæsar

Are we all ready? What is now amiss
That Cæsar and his senate must redress?                    35

Metellus

Most high, most mighty and most puissant Cæsar,
Metellus Cimber throws before thy seat
An humble heart—

[Kneeling.

Cæsar

I must prevent thee, Cimber.
These couchings and these lowly courtesies              40
Might fire the blood of ordinary men,
And turn pre-ordinance and first decree
Into the law of children. Be not fond,
To think that Cæsar bears such rebel blood
That will be thaw'd from the true quality                  45
With that which melteth fools, I mean, sweet words,
Low-crooked curtsies and base spaniel-fawning.
Thy brother by decree is banished:
If thou dost bend and pray and fawn for him,
I spurn thee like a cur out of my way.                      50
Know, Cæsar doth not wrong, nor without cause
Will he be satisfied.

Metellus

Is there no voice more worthy than my own,
To sound more sweetly in great Cæsar's ear
For the repealing of my banish'd brother?                  55

Brutus

I kiss thy hand, but not in flattery, Cæsar,
Desiring thee that Publius Cimber may
Have an immediate freedom of repeal.

Cæsar

What, Brutus!

74 **holds on his rank** continues on his course.

82 **bootless** uselessly.

84 **Et tu, Brute?** "Thou also, Brutus?"

*Cassius*

          Pardon, Cæsar; Cæsar, pardon:     60
  As low as to thy foot doth Cassius fall,
  To beg enfranchisement for Publius Cimber.

*Cæsar*

  I could be well mov'd, if I were as you;
  If I could pray to move, prayers would move me:
  But I am constant as the northern star,     65
  Of whose true-fix'd and resting quality
  There is no fellow in the firmament.
  The skies are painted with unnumber'd sparks;
  They are all fire and every one doth shine;
  But there's but one in all doth hold his place:     70
  So in the world; 'tis furnish'd well with men,
  And men are flesh and blood, and apprehensive;
  Yet in the number I do know but one
  That unassailable holds on his rank,
  Unshak'd of motion: and that I am he,     75
  Let me a little show it, even in this;
  That I was constant Cimber should be banish'd,
  And constant do remain to keep him so.

*Cinna*

  O Cæsar—

*Cæsar*

          Hence! wilt thou lift up Olympus?     80

*Decius*

  Great Cæsar—

*Cæsar*

          Doth not Brutus bootless kneel?

*Casca*

  Speak, hands, for me!
    [*Casca first, then the other conspirators and
             Marcus Brutus stab Cæsar.*

*Cæsar*

  Et tu, Brute? Then fall, Cæsar!
                      [*Dies.*

94 **confounded**   confused.

102 **abide**   suffer for.

*Cinna*
    Liberty! freedom! Tyranny is dead!                              85
    Run hence, proclaim, cry it about the streets.

*Cassius*
    Some to the common pulpits, and cry out
    "Liberty, freedom and enfranchisement!"

*Brutus*
    People, and senators, be not affrighted;
    Fly not; stand still: ambition's debt is paid.                  90

*Casca*
    Go to the pulpit, Brutus.

*Decius*
                           And Cassius too.

*Brutus*
    Where's Publius?

*Cinna*
    Here, quite confounded with this mutiny.

*Metellus*
    Stand fast together, lest some friend of Cæsar's               95
    Should chance—

*Brutus*
    Talk not of standing. Publius, good cheer;
    There is no harm intended to your person,
    Nor to no Roman else: so tell them, Publius.

*Cassius*
    And leave us, Publius; lest that the people                    100
    Rushing on us should do your age some mischief.

*Brutus*
    Do so: and let no man abide this deed
    But we the doers.

    *Reenter Trebonius.*

*Cassius*
    Where is Antony?

*Trebonius*
                     Fled to his house amaz'd:                105

110 **stand upon** care or worry about.

124 **sport** dramatic performance.
125 **basis** the base of the statue.

132 **grace** dignify.

Men, wives and children stare, cry out and run
As it were doomsday.

**Brutus**

　　　　　　Fates, we will know your pleasures:
That we shall die, we know; 'tis but the time,
And drawing days out, that men stand upon.　　　110

**Cassius**

Why, he that cuts off twenty years of life
Cuts off so many years of fearing death.

**Brutus**

Grant that, and then is death a benefit:
So are we Cæsar's friends, that have abridg'd
His time of fearing death. Stoop, Romans, stoop,　　115
And let us bathe our hands in Cæsar's blood
Up to the elbows, and besmear our swords:
Then walk we forth, even to the market-place,
And waving our red weapons o'er our heads,
Let's all cry "Peace, freedom and liberty!"　　　120

**Cassius**

Stoop then, and wash. How many ages hence
Shall this our lofty scene be acted over
In states unborn and accents yet unknown!

**Brutus**

How many times shall Cæsar bleed in sport,
That now on Pompey's basis lies along　　　125
No worthier than the dust!

**Cassius**

　　　　　　So oft as that shall be,
So often shall the knot of us be call'd
The men that gave their country liberty.

**Decius**

What, shall we forth?　　　130

**Cassius**

　　　　　　Aye, every man away:
Brutus shall lead, and we will grace his heels
With the most boldest and best hearts of Rome.

143 **resolv'd** convinced.


148 **thorough** through.
**untrod state** new government.




155 **presently** immediately.




158 **still** always.
159 **falls shrewdly** happens to an extreme degree. Therefore,
"My suspicions unfortunately are always accurate."

*Enter a Servant.*

**Brutus**
Soft! who comes here? A friend of Antony's.

**Servant**
Thus, Brutus, did my master bid me kneel;                    135
Thus did Mark Antony bid me fall down;
And, being prostrate, thus he bade me say:
Brutus is noble, wise, valiant and honest;
Cæsar was mighty, bold, royal and loving:
Say I love Brutus and I honor him;                           140
Say I fear'd Cæsar, honor'd him and lov'd him.
If Brutus will vouchsafe that Antony
May safely come to him and be resolv'd
How Cæsar hath deserv'd to lie in death,
Mark Antony shall not love Cæsar dead                        145
So well as Brutus living, but will follow
The fortunes and affairs of noble Brutus
Thorough the hazards of this untrod state
With all true faith. So says my master Antony.

**Brutus**
Thy master is a wise and valiant Roman;                      150
I never thought him worse.
Tell him, so please him come unto this place,
He shall be satisfied and, by my honor,
Depart untouch'd.

**Servant**
                    I'll fetch him presently.                155
                                              [*Exit.*

**Brutus**
I know that we shall have him well to friend.

**Cassius**
I wish we may: but yet have I a mind
That fears him much, and my misgivings still
Falls shrewdly to the purpose.

   *Reenter Antony.*

165 **rank**   offensive.

171 **purpled**   blood-stained.

186 **leaden points**   blunted, not dangerous.

191 **new dignities**   political patronage.

*Brutus*

    But here comes Antony. Welcome, Mark Antony.     160

*Antony*

    O mighty Cæsar! dost thou lie so low?
    Are all thy conquests, glories, triumphs, spoils,
    Shrunk to this little measure? Fare thee well.
    I know not, gentlemen, what you intend,
    Who else must be let blood, who else is rank:     165
    If I myself, there is no hour so fit
    As Cæsar's death's hour, nor no instrument
    Of half that worth as those your swords, made rich
    With the most noble blood of all this world.
    I do beseech ye, if you bear me hard,     170
    Now, whilst your purpled hands do reek and smoke,
    Fulfill your pleasure. Live a thousand years,
    I shall not find myself so apt to die:
    No place will please me so, no mean of death,
    As here by Cæsar, and by you cut off,     175
    The choice and master spirits of this age.

*Brutus*

    O Antony, beg not your death of us.
    Though now we must appear bloody and cruel,
    As, by our hands and this our present act,
    You see we do; yet see you but our hands     180
    And this the bleeding business they have done:
    Our hearts you see not; they are pitiful;
    And pity to the general wrong of Rome—
    As fire drives out fire, so pity pity—
    Hath done this deed on Cæsar. For your part,     185
    To you our swords have leaden points, Mark Antony:
    Our arms in strength of malice, and our hearts
    Of brothers' temper, do receive you in
    With all kind love, good thoughts and reverence.

*Cassius*

    Your voice shall be as strong as any man's     190
    In the disposing of new dignities.

205 **credit**  reputation.
206 **conceit**  see, regard.


210 **dearer**  more intensely.


213 **corse**  corpse.


218 **bay'd**  hunted to death.

220 **sign'd in thy spoil**  marked with the signs of Cæsar's destruction.
**crimson'd in thy Lethe**  bloodied in the act which had brought Cæsar oblivion. Lethe was the name of the river of forgetfulness through which the souls of the dead passed on their way to Hades.

*Brutus*

　　Only be patient till we have appeas'd
　　The multitude, beside themselves with fear,
　　And then we will deliver you the cause
　　Why I, that did love Cæsar when I struck him,　　195
　　Have thus proceeded.

*Antony*

　　　　　　　　I doubt not of your wisdom.
　　Let each man render me his bloody hand:
　　First, Marcus Brutus, will I shake with you;
　　Next, Caius Cassius, do I take your hand;　　200
　　Now, Decius Brutus, yours; now yours, Metellus;
　　Yours, Cinna; and, my valiant Casca, yours;
　　Though last, not least in love, yours, good Trebonius.
　　Gentlemen all—alas, what shall I say?
　　My credit now stands on such slippery ground,　　205
　　That one of two bad ways you must conceit me,
　　Either a coward or a flatterer.
　　That I did love thee, Cæsar, O, 'tis true:
　　If then thy spirit look upon us now,
　　Shall it not grieve thee dearer than thy death,　　210
　　To see thy Antony making his peace,
　　Shaking the bloody fingers of thy foes,
　　Most noble! in the presence of thy corse?
　　Had I as many eyes as thou hast wounds,
　　Weeping as fast as they stream forth thy blood,　　215
　　It would become me better than to close
　　In terms of friendship with thine enemies.
　　Pardon me, Julius! Here wast thou bay'd, brave heart;
　　Here didst thou fall, and here thy hunters stand,
　　Sign'd in thy spoil and crimson'd in thy lethe.　　220
　　O world, thou wast the forest to this hart;
　　And this, indeed, O world, the heart of thee.
　　How like a deer strucken by many princes
　　Dost thou here lie!

*Cassius*

　　Mark Antony—　　　　　　　　　　　　225

228 **cold modesty**  dispassionate understatement.

231 **prick'd**  marked on a list.

239 **good regard**  sound quality.

244 **produce**  convey.

246 **order**  course.

*Antony*
                   Pardon me, Caius Cassius:
  The enemies of Cæsar shall say this;
  Then, in a friend, it is cold modesty.

*Cassius*
  I blame you not for praising Cæsar so;
  But what compact mean you to have with us?                    230
  Will you be prick'd in number of our friends,
  Or shall we on, and not depend on you?

*Antony*
  Therefore I took your hands, but was indeed
  Sway'd from the point by looking down on Cæsar.
  Friends am I with you all and love you all,                    235
  Upon this hope that you shall give me reasons
  Why and wherein Cæsar was dangerous.

*Brutus*
  Or else were this a savage spectacle:
  Our reasons are so full of good regard
  That were you, Antony, the son of Cæsar,                       240
  You should be satisfied.

*Antony*
                    That's all I seek:
  And am moreover suitor that I may
  Produce his body to the market-place,
  And in the pulpit, as becomes a friend,                        245
  Speak in the order of his funeral.

*Brutus*
  You shall, Mark Antony.

*Cassius*
               Brutus, a word with you.
    [*Aside to Brutus*]
  You know not what you do: do not consent
  That Antony speak in his funeral:                              250
  Know you how much the people may be mov'd
  By that which he will utter?

260 **advantage**   help.

261 **fall**   happen, befall.

279 **ope**   open.

*Brutus*
                              By your pardon:
I will myself into the pulpit first,
And show the reason of our Cæsar's death:          255
What Antony shall speak, I will protest
He speaks by leave and by permission,
And that we are contented Cæsar shall
Have all true rites and lawful ceremonies.
It shall advantage more than do us wrong.          260

*Cassius*
I know not what may fall; I like it not.

*Brutus*
Mark Antony, here, take you Cæsar's body.
You shall not in your funeral speech blame us,
But speak all good you can devise of Cæsar,
And say you do 't by our permission;               265
Else shall you not have any hand at all
About his funeral: and you shall speak
In the same pulpit whereto I am going,
After my speech is ended.

*Antony*
                              Be it so;             270
I do desire no more.

*Brutus*
Prepare the body then, and follow us.
                    [*Exeunt all but Antony.*

*Antony*
O, pardon me, thou bleeding piece of earth,
That I am meek and gentle with these butchers!
Thou art the ruins of the noblest man              275
That ever lived in the tide of times.
Woe to the hand that shed this costly blood!
Over thy wounds now do I prophesy,
Which like dumb mouths do ope their ruby lips
To beg the voice and utterance of my tongue,       280
A curse shall light upon the limbs of men;

283 **cumber**  weigh down.

288 **custom of fell deeds**  familiarity with cruel and dreadful deeds.
290 **Ate**  goddess personifying the fatal qualities which produce crime and the divine punishment which follows it.
292 **Havoc**  a word used as the signal for complete and merciless destruction in warfare.
**let slip**  release.
**the dogs of war**  the forces of war.

Domestic fury and fierce civil strife
Shall cumber all the parts of Italy;
Blood and destruction shall be so in use,
And dreadful objects so familiar,                              285
That mothers shall but smile when they behold
Their infants quarter'd with the hands of war;
All pity chok'd with custom of fell deeds:
And Cæsar's spirit ranging for revenge,
With Ate by his side come hot from hell,                       290
Shall in these confines with a monarch's voice
Cry "Havoc," and let slip the dogs of war;
That this foul deed shall smell above the earth
With carrion men, groaning for burial.

    *Enter a Servant.*

You serve Octavius Cæsar, do you not?                          295
*Servant*
  I do, Mark Antony.
*Antony*
  Cæsar did write for him to come to Rome.
*Servant*
  He did receive his letters, and is coming;
  And bid me say to you by word of mouth—
  O Cæsar!                                                     300
                    *[Seeing the body.*
*Antony*
  Thy heart is big; get thee apart and weep.
  Passion, I see, is catching, for mine eyes,
  Seeing those beads of sorrow stand in thine,
  Began to water. Is thy master coming?
*Servant*
  He lies tonight within seven leagues of Rome.                305
*Antony*
  Post back with speed, and tell him what hath chanc'd:
  Here is a mourning Rome, a dangerous Rome,
  No Rome of safety for Octavius yet;

310 **corse** corpse.

313 **issue** results.

11 **severally** separately.

Hie hence, and tell him so. Yet stay awhile;
Thou shalt not back till I have borne this corse      310
Into the market-place: there shall I try,
In my oration, how the people take
The cruel issue of these bloody men;
According to the which, thou shalt discourse
To young Octavius of the state of things.      315
Lend me your hand.

*[Exeunt with Cæsar's body.*


*Scene 2. The Forum*

*Enter Brutus and Cassius, and a throng of Citizens.*

**Citizens**
We will be satisfied; let us be satisfied.

**Brutus**
Then follow me, and give me audience, friends.
Cassius, go you into the other street,
And part the numbers.
Those that will hear me speak, let 'em stay here;      5
Those that will follow Cassius, go with him;
And public reasons shall be rendered
Of Cæsar's death.

**First Citizen**
I will hear Brutus speak.

**Second Citizen**
I will hear Cassius; and compare their reasons,      10
When severally we hear them rendered.

*[Exit Cassius, with some of the Citizens.*
*Brutus goes into the pulpit.*

**Third Citizen**
The noble Brutus is ascended: silence!

14 **lovers** dear friends.

17 **censure** judge.

39 **extenuated** made little of.
40 **enforced** exaggerated.

*Brutus*

Be patient till the last.

Romans, countrymen, and lovers! hear me for my
cause, and be silent, that you may hear: believe me    15
for mine honor, and have respect to mine honor, that
you may believe: censure me in your wisdom, and
awake your senses, that you may the better judge. If
there be any in this assembly, any dear friend of
Cæsar's, to him I say that Brutus' love to Caesar was    20
no less than his. If then that friend demand why
Brutus rose against Cæsar, this is my answer: not that
I loved Cæsar less, but that I loved Rome more. Had
you rather Cæsar were living, and die all slaves, than
that Cæsar were dead, to live all freemen? As Cæsar    25
loved me, I weep for him; as he was fortunate, I rejoice at it; as he was valiant, I honor him; but as he
was ambitious, I slew him. There is tears for his love;
joy for his fortune; honor for his valor; and death
for his ambition. Who is here so base that would be    30
a bondman? If any, speak; for him have I offended.
Who is here so rude that would not be a Roman? If
any, speak; for him have I offended. Who is here so
vile that will not love his country? If any, speak; for
him have I offended. I pause for a reply.    35

*All*

None, Brutus, none.

*Brutus*

Then none have I offended. I have done no more to
Cæsar than you shall do to Brutus. The question of
his death is enrolled in the Capitol; his glory not extenuated, wherein he was worthy, nor his offenses en-    40
forced, for which he suffered death.

*Enter Antony and others, with Cæsar's body.*

Here comes his body, mourned by Mark Antony: who,
though he had no hand in his death, shall receive the

52 **Let him be Cæsar**  possibly, let him take Cæsar's place. The word *Cæsar* had not yet become a title denoting *ruler* (as it did in the time of Augustus). Subsequently, of course, the title passed into many languages: *kaiser, czar,* etc.

61 **grace**  used here both as a noun and a verb with the meaning of *respect.*

65 **save**  except.

benefit of his dying, a place in the commonwealth;
as which of you shall not? With this I depart—that,    45
as I slew my best lover for the good of Rome, I have
the same dagger for myself, when it shall please my
country to need my death.

*All*
Live, Brutus! live, live!

*First Citizen*
Bring him with triumph home unto his house.    50

*Second Citizen*
Give him a statue with his ancestors.

*Third Citizen*
Let him be Cæsar.

*Fourth Citizen*
                    Cæsar's better parts
Shall be crown'd in Brutus.

*First Citizen*
We'll bring him to his house with shouts and clamors.    55

*Brutus*
My countrymen—

*Second Citizen*
                    Peace! silence! Brutus speaks.

*First Citizen*
Peace, ho!

*Brutus*
Good countrymen, let me depart alone,
And, for my sake, stay here with Antony:    60
Do grace to Cæsar's corpse, and grace his speech
Tending to Cæsar's glories, which Mark Antony
By our permission is allow'd to make.
I do entreat you, not a man depart,
Save I alone, till Antony have spoke.    65
                                        [*Exit.*

*First Citizen*
Stay, ho! and let us hear Mark Antony.

69 **beholding**   indebted.

78 **gentle Romans**   gentlemen of Rome.

87 **answer'd**   paid for.

**Third Citizen**

    Let him go up into the public chair;
    We'll hear him. Noble Antony, go up.

**Antony**

    For Brutus' sake, I am beholding to you.

                        [*Goes into the pulpit.*

**Fourth Citizen**

    What does he say of Brutus?                                70

**Third Citizen**

                    He says, for Brutus' sake,
    He finds himself beholding to us all.

**Fourth Citizen**

    'Twere best he speak no harm of Brutus here.

**First Citizen**

    This Cæsar was a tyrant.

**Third Citizen**

                      Nay, that's certain:                    75
    We are blest that Rome is rid of him.

**Second Citizen**

    Peace! let us hear what Antony can say.

**Antony**

    You gentle Romans—

**All**

                  Peace, ho! let us hear him.

**Antony**

    Friends, Romans, countrymen, lend me your ears;     80
    I come to bury Cæsar, not to praise him.
    The evil that men do lives after them;
    The good is oft interred with their bones;
    So let it be with Cæsar. The noble Brutus
    Hath told you Cæsar was ambitious:                  85
    If it were so, it was a grievous fault,
    And grievously hath Cæsar answer'd it.
    Here, under leave of Brutus and the rest—
    For Brutus is an honorable man;

96 **general coffers**   public treasury.

So are they all, all honorable men—                    90
Come I to speak in Cæsar's funeral.
He was my friend, faithful and just to me:
But Brutus says he was ambitious;
And Brutus is an honorable man.
He hath brought many captives home to Rome,          95
Whose ransoms did the general coffers fill:
Did this in Cæsar seem ambitious?
When that the poor have cried, Cæsar hath wept:
Ambition should be made of sterner stuff:
Yet Brutus says he was ambitious;                    100
And Brutus is an honorable man.
You all did see that on the Lupercal
I thrice presented him a kingly crown,
Which he did thrice refuse: was this ambition?
Yet Brutus says he was ambitious,                    105
And, sure, he is an honorable man.
I speak not to disprove what Brutus spoke,
But here I am to speak what I do know.
You all did love him once, not without cause:
What cause withholds you then to mourn for him?      110
O judgment! thou art fled to brutish beasts,
And men have lost their reason. Bear with me;
My heart is in the coffin there with Cæsar,
And I must pause till it come back to me.

*First Citizen*
Methinks there is much reason in his sayings.        115

*Second Citizen*
If thou consider rightly of the matter,
Cæsar has had great wrong.

*Third Citizen*
                              Has he, masters?
I fear there will a worse come in his place.

*Fourth Citizen*
Mark'd ye his words? He would not take the crown;    120
Therefore 'tis certain he was not ambitious.

**122 dear abide it**   If Cæsar is proved not ambitious, his assassins will pay for their crime.

**145 issue**   children, heirs.

*First Citizen*
  If it be found so, some will dear abide it.
*Second Citizen*
  Poor soul! his eyes are red as fire with weeping.
*Third Citizen*
  There's not a nobler man in Rome than Antony.
*Fourth Citizen*
  Now mark him, he begins again to speak.     125
*Antony*
  But yesterday the word of Cæsar might
  Have stood against the world: now lies he there,
  And none so poor to do him reverence.
  O masters, if I were dispos'd to stir
  Your hearts and minds to mutiny and rage,     130
  I should do Brutus wrong and Cassius wrong,
  Who, you all know, are honorable men:
  I will not do them wrong; I rather choose
  To wrong the dead, to wrong myself and you,
  Than I will wrong such honorable men.     135
  But here's a parchment with the seal of Cæsar;
  I found it in his closet; 'tis his will:
  Let but the commons hear this testament—
  Which, pardon me, I do not mean to read—
  And they would go and kiss dead Cæsar's wounds     140
  And dip their napkins in his sacred blood,
  Yea, beg a hair of him for memory,
  And, dying, mention it within their wills,
  Bequeathing it as a rich legacy
  Unto their issue.     145
*Fourth Citizen*
  We'll hear the will: read it, Mark Antony.
*All*
  The will, the will! we will hear Cæsar's will.
*Antony*
  Have patience, gentle friends, I must not read it;
  It is not meet you know how Cæsar lov'd you.

**158 o'ershot** gone beyond my abilities.

You are not wood, you are not stones, but men;                150
And, being men, hearing the will of Cæsar,
It will inflame you, it will make you mad:
'Tis good you know not that you are his heirs;
For if you should, O, what would come of it!

*Fourth Citizen*
Read the will; we'll hear it, Antony;                         155
You shall read us the will, Cæsar's will.

*Antony*
Will you be patient? will you stay awhile?
I have o'ershot myself to tell you of it:
I fear I wrong the honorable men
Whose daggers have stabb'd Cæsar; I do fear it.              160

*Fourth Citizen*
They were traitors: honorable men!

*All*
The will! the testament!

*Second Citizen*
They were villains, murderers: the will! read the will.

*Antony*
You will compel me then to read the will?
Then make a ring about the corpse of Cæsar,                  165
And let me show you him that made the will.
Shall I descend? and will you give me leave?

*All*
Come down.

*Second Citizen*
Descend.
                    [*He comes down from the pulpit.*

*Third Citizen*
You shall have leave.                                        170

*Fourth Citizen*
A ring! stand round.

*First Citizen*
Stand from the hearse, stand from the body.

180 **Nervii**  one of the tribes defeated by Cæsar during his conquest of Gaul.

203 **vesture**  clothing.

**Second Citizen**
　　Room for Antony, most noble Antony.
**Antony**
　　Nay, press not so upon me; stand far off.
**All**
　　Stand back. Room! Bear back.　　　　　　　　175
**Antony**
　　If you have tears, prepare to shed them now.
　　You all do know this mantle: I remember
　　The first time ever Cæsar put it on;
　　'Twas on a summer's evening, in his tent,
　　That day he overcame the Nervii:　　　　　180
　　Look, in this place ran Cassius' dagger through:
　　See what a rent the envious Casca made:
　　Through this the well-beloved Brutus stabb'd;
　　And as he pluck'd his cursed steel away,
　　Mark how the blood of Cæsar follow'd it,　　185
　　As rushing out of doors, to be resolv'd
　　If Brutus so unkindly knock'd, or no:
　　For Brutus, as you know, was Cæsar's angel:
　　Judge, O you gods, how dearly Cæsar lov'd him!
　　This was the most unkindest cut of all;　　190
　　For when the noble Cæsar saw him stab,
　　Ingratitude, more strong than traitors' arms,
　　Quite vanquish'd him: then burst his mighty heart;
　　And, in his mantle muffling up his face,
　　Even at the base of Pompey's statuë,　　　195
　　Which all the while ran blood, great Cæsar fell.
　　O, what a fall was there, my countrymen!
　　Then I, and you, and all of us fell down,
　　Whilst bloody treason flourish'd over us.
　　O, now you weep, and I perceive you feel　　200
　　The dint of pity: these are gracious drops.
　　Kind souls, what weep you when you but behold
　　Our Cæsar's vesture wounded? Look you here,
　　Here is himself, marr'd, as you see, with traitors.

223 **no orator**   Plutarch said of Antony, "He took most to what was called the Asiatic taste in speaking, which was . . . full of empty flourishes and unsteady efforts for glory." Shakespeare's Antony is obviously a consummate orator and aware both of that fact and of the necessity to present himself to the people as a "plain, blunt man."

227 **wit**   understanding.

*First Citizen*
   O piteous spectacle!                                      205

*Second Citizen*
   O noble Cæsar!

*Third Citizen*
   O woeful day!

*Fourth Citizen*
   O traitors, villains!

*First Citizen*
   O most bloody sight!

*Second Citizen*
   We will be revenged.                                     210

*All*
   Revenge! About! Seek! Burn! Fire! Kill! Slay! Let not
   a traitor live!

*Antony*
   Stay, countrymen.

*First Citizen*
   Peace there! hear the noble Antony.

*Second Citizen*
   We'll hear him, we'll follow him, we'll die with him.   215

*Antony*
   Good friends, sweet friends, let me not stir you up
   To such a sudden flood of mutiny.
   They that have done this deed are honorable;
   What private griefs they have, alas, I know not,
   That made them do it: they are wise and honorable,   220
   And will, no doubt, with reasons answer you.
   I come not, friends, to steal away your hearts:
   I am no orator, as Brutus is;
   But, as you know me all, a plain blunt man,
   That love my friend; and that they know full well   225
   That gave me public leave to speak of him:
   For I have neither wit, nor words, nor worth,
   Action, nor utterance, nor the power of speech,
   To stir men's blood: I only speak right on;

234 **ruffle up**   make furious.

249 **drachmas**   Greek coins (of slight value).

I tell you that which you yourselves do know;     230
Show you sweet Cæsar's wounds, poor poor dumb
    mouths,
And bid them speak for me: but were I Brutus,
And Brutus Antony, there were an Antony
Would ruffle up your spirits, and put a tongue
In every wound of Cæsar, that should move     235
The stones of Rome to rise and mutiny.

*All*

We'll mutiny.

*First Citizen*

             We'll burn the house of Brutus.

*Third Citizen*

Away, then! come, seek the conspirators.

*Antony*

Yet hear me, countrymen: yet hear me speak.     240

*All*

Peace, ho! Hear Antony. Most noble Antony!

*Antony*

Why, friends, you go to do you know not what:
Wherein hath Cæsar thus deserv'd your loves?
Alas, you know not; I must tell you then:
You have forgot the will I told you of.     245

*All*

Most true: the will! Let's stay and hear the will.

*Antony*

Here is the will, and under Cæsar's seal.
To every Roman citizen he gives,
To every several man, seventy-five drachmas.

*Second Citizen*

Most noble Cæsar! we'll revenge his death.     250

*Third Citizen*

O royal Cæsar!

*Antony*

           Hear me with patience.

257 **common pleasures** pleasure gardens for the general public.

266 **forms** benches.

267 **afoot** unleashed, made active.

*All*
  Peace, ho!
*Antony*
  Moreover, he hath left you all his walks,
  His private arbors and new-planted orchards,            255
  On this side Tiber; he hath left them you,
  And to your heirs for ever; common pleasures,
  To walk abroad and recreate yourselves.
  Here was a Cæsar! when comes such another?
*First Citizen*
  Never, never. Come, away, away!            260
  We'll burn his body in the holy place,
  And with the brands fire the traitors' houses.
  Take up the body.
*Second Citizen*
  Go fetch fire.
*Third Citizen*
  Pluck down benches.            265
*Fourth Citizen*
  Pluck down forms, windows, any thing.
                    [*Exeunt Citizens with the body.*
*Antony*
  Now let it work. Mischief, thou art afoot,
  Take thou what course thou wilt.

        *Enter a Servant.*

                          How now, fellow!
*Servant*
  Sir, Octavius is already come to Rome.            270
*Antony*
  Where is he?
*Servant*
  He and Lepidus are at Cæsar's house.
*Antony*
  And thither will I straight to visit him.

274 **upon a wish**   just when he is wanted.

278 **Belike**   probably, perhaps.

2 **unluckily charge my fantasy**   bad omens disturb my imagination.

He comes upon a wish. Fortune is merry,
And in this mood will give us any thing.                    275

*Servant*

I heard him say, Brutus and Cassius
Are rid like madmen through the gates of Rome.

*Antony*

Belike they had some notice of the people,
How I had moved them. Bring me to Octavius.

                    [*Exeunt.*


## Scene 3. A street

*Enter Cinna the poet.*


*Cinna*

I dreamt tonight that I did feast with Cæsar,
And things unluckily charge my fantasy:
I have no will to wander forth of doors,
Yet something leads me forth.

    *Enter Citizens.*

*First Citizen*

What is your name?                                          5

*Second Citizen*

Whither are you going?

*Third Citizen*

Where do you dwell?

*Fourth Citizen*

Are you a married man or a bachelor?

*Second Citizen*

Answer every man directly.

*First Citizen*

Aye, and briefly.                                           10

12 **you were best**  you had better.

18 **bear me a bang**  get a blow from me.

*Fourth Citizen*
Aye, and wisely.

*Third Citizen*
Aye, and truly, you were best.

*Cinna*
What is my name? Whither am I going? Where do
I dwell? Am I a married man or a bachelor? Then,
to answer every man directly and briefly, wisely and     15
truly: wisely I say, I am a bachelor.

*Second Citizen*
That's as much as to say, they are fools that marry:
you'll bear me a bang for that, I fear. Proceed: directly.

*Cinna*
Directly, I am going to Cæsar's funeral.

*First Citizen*
As a friend or an enemy?     20

*Cinna*
As a friend.

*Second Citizen*
That matter is answered directly.

*Fourth Citizen*
For your dwelling, briefly.

*Cinna*
Briefly, I dwell by the Capitol.

*Third Citizen*
Your name, sir, truly.     25

*Cinna*
Truly, my name is Cinna.

*First Citizen*
Tear him to pieces; he's a conspirator.

*Cinna*
I am Cinna the poet, I am Cinna the poet.

*Fourth Citizen*
Tear him for his bad verses, tear him for his bad
verses.     30

34 **fire-brands** sticks or stakes that can be set aflame.

1 **prick'd** marked with a dot (in this case, for death).

*Cinna*

   I am not Cinna the conspirator.

*Fourth Citizen*

   It is no matter, his name's Cinna; pluck but his name
   out of his heart, and turn him going.

*Third Citizen*

   Tear him, tear him! Come, brands, ho! fire-brands:
   to Brutus', to Cassius'; burn all: some to Decius'    35
   house, and some to Casca's; some to Ligarius': away,
   go!

                                          *[Exeunt.*

# ACT IV

### Scene 1. A house in Rome

*Antony, Octavius, and Lepidus, seated at a table.*

*Antony*

   These many then shall die; their names are prick'd.

*Octavius*

   Your brother too must die; consent you, Lepidus?

*Lepidus*

   I do consent—

*Octavius*

              Prick him down, Antony.

*Lepidus*

   Upon condition Publius shall not live,
   Who is your sister's son, Mark Antony.

*Antony*

   He shall not live; look, with a spot I damn him.

10 **cut off some charge**   reduce the expense of.

14 **meet**   suited.

18 **proscription**   condemning to death.

22 **divers**   various.

29 **commons**   general fields.

33 **store of provender**   food for cattle.

But, Lepidus, go you to Cæsar's house;
Fetch the will hither, and we shall determine
How to cut off some charge in legacies.            10

Lepidus
What, shall I find you here?

Octavius
Or here, or at the Capitol.

                    [*Exit Lepidus.*

Antony
This is a slight unmeritable man,
Meet to be sent on errands: is it fit,
The three-fold world divided, he should stand     15
One of the three to share it?

Octavius
                  So you thought him,
And took his voice who should be prick'd to die
In our black sentence and proscription.

Antony
Octavius, I have seen more days than you:          20
And though we lay these honors on this man,
To ease ourselves of divers sland'rous loads,
He shall but bear them as the ass bears gold,
To groan and sweat under the business,
Either led or driven, as we point the way;         25
And having brought our treasure where we will,
Then take we down his load and turn him off,
Like to the empty ass, to shake his ears
And graze in commons.

Octavius
                You may do your will:         30
But he's a tried and valiant soldier.

Antony
So is my horse, Octavius, and for that
I do appoint him store of provender:
It is a creature that I teach to fight,

35 **wind**   to recover breath after exertion.

37 **taste**   degree, respect.


40 **abjects, orts**   worthless scraps.
41 **stal'd**   cheapened by overuse.

43 **property**   thing for our use.

45 **make head**   assemble our forces.


49 **covert matters may be best disclos'd**   enemy secrets may
be best discovered.

51 **at the stake**   in danger.


Stage directions **Sardis**   the capital of Lydia, in Asia Minor.

To wind, to stop, to run directly on,                          35
His corporal motion govern'd by my spirit.
And, in some taste, is Lepidus but so;
He must be taught, and train'd, and bid go forth;
A barren-spirited fellow; one that feeds
On abjects, orts and imitations,                               40
Which, out of use and stal'd by other men,
Begin his fashion: do not talk of him
But as a property. And now, Octavius,
Listen great things: Brutus and Cassius
Are levying powers: we must straight make head:                45
Therefore let our alliance be combined,
Our best friends made, our means stretch'd;
And let us presently go sit in council,
How covert matters may be best disclos'd,
And open perils surest answered.                               50

*Octavius*
Let us do so: for we are at the stake,
And bay'd about with many enemies;
And some that smile have in their hearts, I fear,
Millions of mischiefs.

                                    [*Exeunt.*


*Scene 2. Camp near Sardis. Before Brutus's tent*

*Drum. Enter Brutus, Lucilius, Lucius, and Soldiers;
Titinius and Pindarus meet them.*

*Brutus*
Stand, ho!

*Lucilius*
Give the word, ho! and stand!

*Brutus*
What now, Lucilius! is Cassius near?

6 **He greets me well**   a worthy man brings me his greetings.
7 **In his own change, or by ill officers**   either because he has changed or his officers have incorrectly carried out his instructions.

17 **familiar instances**   friendly indications.

23 **enforced**   forced, assumed.

25 **hot at hand**   spirited when halted or checked.

28 **fall their crests**   drop their necks.
    **jades**   horses of inferior breed.
29 **sink in the trial**   fail under fire.

*Lucilius*

    He is at hand; and Pindarus is come
    To do you salutation from his master.           5

*Brutus*

    He greets me well. Your master, Pindarus,
    In his own change, or by ill officers,
    Hath given me some worthy cause to wish
    Things done undone: but if he be at hand,
    I shall be satisfied.           10

*Pindarus*

              I do not doubt
    But that my noble master will appear
    Such as he is, full of regard and honor.

*Brutus*

    He is not doubted. A word, Lucilius,
    How he receiv'd you: let me be resolv'd.      15

*Lucilius*

    With courtesy and with respect enough,
    But not with such familiar instances,
    Nor with such free and friendly conference,
    As he hath used of old.

*Brutus*

              Thou hast describ'd    20
    A hot friend cooling: ever note, Lucilius,
    When love begins to sicken and decay,
    It useth an enforced ceremony.
    There are no tricks in plain and simple faith:
    But hollow men, like horses hot at hand,    25
    Make gallant show and promise of their mettle;
    But when they should endure the bloody spur,
    They fall their crests and like deceitful jades
    Sink in the trial. Comes his army on?

*Lucilius*

    They mean this night in Sardis to be quarter'd;    30
    The greater part, the horse in general,
    Are come with Cassius.

                    [*Low march within.*

45 **be content**   be calm.

50 **griefs**   complaints, reasons for feeling aggrieved.

*Brutus*
>                        Hark! he is arriv'd:
> March gently on to meet him.

>    *Enter Cassius and his powers.*

*Cassius*
> Stand, ho!                                    35
*Brutus*
> Stand, ho! Speak the word along.
*First Soldier*
> Stand!
*Second Soldier*
> Stand!
*Third Soldier*
> Stand!
*Cassius*
> Most noble brother, you have done me wrong.    40
*Brutus*
> Judge me, you gods! wrong I mine enemies?
> And, if not so, how should I wrong a brother?

*Cassius*
> Brutus, this sober form of yours hides wrongs;
> And when you do them—

*Brutus*
>                        Cassius, be content;    45
> Speak your griefs softly: I do know you well.
> Before the eyes of both our armies here,
> Which should perceive nothing but love from us,
> Let us not wrangle: bid them move away;
> Then in my tent, Cassius, enlarge your griefs,    50
> And I will give you audience.

*Cassius*
>                        Pindarus,
> Bid our commanders lead their charges off
> A little from this ground.

2 **noted**   disgraced.

8 **nice**   slight.
   **bear his comment**   be noted.
10 **condemn'd to have**   judged as having.
   **an itching palm**   a too great love of money.
11 **mart**   trade.

17 **chastisement**   punishment.

*Brutus*

Lucilius, do you the like, and let no man                    55
Come to our tent till we have done our conference.
Let Lucius and Titinius guard our door.

[*Exeunt.*


## Scene 3. *Brutus's tent*

~~~~~~~~~~~~~~~~~~~~~~

*Enter Brutus and Cassius.*

*Cassius*

That you have wrong'd me doth appear in this:
You have condemn'd and noted Lucius Pella
For taking bribes here of the Sardians;
Wherein my letters, praying on his side,
Because I knew the man, were slighted off.             5

*Brutus*

You wrong'd yourself to write in such a case.

*Cassius*

In such a time as this it is not meet
That every nice offense should bear his comment.

*Brutus*

Let me tell you, Cassius, you yourself
Are much condemn'd to have an itching palm,          10
To sell and mart your offices for gold
To undeservers.

*Cassius*

         I an itching palm!
You know that you are Brutus that speaks this,
Or, by the gods, this speech were else your last.     15

*Brutus*

The name of Cassius honors this corruption,
And chastisement doth therefore hide his head.

21 **villain** Brutus does not mean that those who stabbed Cæsar were villains but that they *would have been* villains if they had stabbed him for any cause except justice.

28 **and bay the moon** proverbially the moon is impervious to the barking of dogs; therefore, the meaning is to proceed with no hope.
30 **bait** worry or harass.

43 **choler** anger.

*Cassius*
  Chastisement!

*Brutus*
  Remember March, the ides of March remember:
  Did not great Julius bleed for justice' sake?          20
  What villain touch'd his body, that did stab,
  And not for justice? What, shall one of us,
  That struck the foremost man of all this world
  But for supporting robbers, shall we now
  Contaminate our fingers with base bribes,          25
  And sell the mighty space of our large honors
  For so much trash as may be grasped thus?
  I had rather be a dog, and bay the moon,
  Than such a Roman.

*Cassius*
                      Brutus, bait not me;          30
  I'll not endure it: you forget yourself,
  To hedge me in; I am a soldier, I,
  Older in practice, abler than yourself
  To make conditions.

*Brutus*
                      Go to; you are not, Cassius.          35

*Cassius*
  I am.

*Brutus*
  I say you are not.

*Cassius*
  Urge me no more, I shall forget myself;
  Have mind upon your health, tempt me no farther.

*Brutus*
  Away, slight man!          40

*Cassius*
  Is 't possible?

*Brutus*
                  Hear me, for I will speak.
  Must I give way and room to your rash choler?
  Shall I be frighted when a madman stares?

**51 digest the venom of your spleen**   contain your own anger.

**64 durst**   dare not.

*Cassius*

    O ye gods, ye gods! must I endure all this?     45

*Brutus*

    All this! aye, more: fret till your proud heart break;
    Go show your slaves how choleric you are,
    And make your bondmen tremble. Must I budge?
    Must I observe you? must I stand and crouch
    Under your testy humor? By the gods,     50
    You shall digest the venom of your spleen,
    Though it do split you; for, from this day forth,
    I'll use you for my mirth, yea, for my laughter,
    When you are waspish.

*Cassius*

               Is it come to this?     55

*Brutus*

    You say you are a better soldier:
    Let it appear so; make your vaunting true,
    And it shall please me well: for mine own part,
    I shall be glad to learn of noble men.

*Cassius*

    You wrong me every way; you wrong me, Brutus;     60
    I said, an elder soldier, not a better:
    Did I say, better?

*Brutus*

          If you did, I care not.

*Cassius*

    When Cæsar liv'd, he durst not thus have mov'd me.

*Brutus*

    Peace, peace! you durst not so have tempted him.     65

*Cassius*

    I durst not!

*Brutus*

    No.

*Cassius*

    What, durst not tempt him!

81 **vile trash**  Brutus, by philosophy a Stoic, despised money.
82 **indirection**  irregular or illegitimate means.

87 **rascal counters**  paltry token coins.

*Brutus*

                    For your life you durst not.

*Cassius*

    Do not presume too much upon my love;       70
    I may do that I shall be sorry for.

*Brutus*

    You have done that you should be sorry for.
    There is no terror, Cassius, in your threats;
    For I am arm'd so strong in honesty,
    That they pass by me as the idle wind       75
    Which I respect not. I did send to you
    For certain sums of gold, which you denied me:
    For I can raise no money by vile means:
    By heaven, I had rather coin my heart,
    And drop my blood for drachmas, than to wring    80
    From the hard hands of peasants their vile trash
    By any indirection. I did send
    To you for gold to pay my legions,
    Which you denied me: was that done like Cassius?
    Should I have answer'd Caius Cassius so?      85
    When Marcus Brutus grows so covetous,
    To lock such rascal counters from his friends,
    Be ready, gods, with all your thunderbolts,
    Dash him to pieces!

*Cassius*

                 I denied you not.      90

*Brutus*

    You did.

*Cassius*

            I did not: he was but a fool
    That brought my answer back. Brutus hath riv'd my
        heart:
    A friend should bear his friend's infirmities,
    But Brutus makes mine greater than they are.    95

*Brutus*

    I do not, till you practise them on me.

105 **brav'd**   challenged.
106 **Check'd**   rebuked.
107 **learn'd and conn'd by rote**   learned by heart.


111 **Pluto**   the god of the underworld, who owned the riches of the mines of the earth.

**Cassius**

You love me not.

**Brutus**

　　　　　　　I do not like your faults.

**Cassius**

A friendly eye could never see such faults.

**Brutus**

A flatterer's would not, though they do appear　　100
As huge as high Olympus.

**Cassius**

Come, Antony, and young Octavius, come,
Revenge yourselves alone on Cassius,
For Cassius is aweary of the world;
Hated by one he loves; brav'd by his brother;　　105
Check'd like a bondman; all his faults observ'd,
Set in a note-book, learn'd and conn'd by rote,
To cast into my teeth. O, I could weep
My spirit from mine eyes! There is my dagger,
And here my naked breast; within, a heart　　110
Dearer than Pluto's mine, richer than gold;
If that thou be'st a Roman, take it forth;
I, that denied thee gold, will give my heart:
Strike, as thou didst at Cæsar; for I know,
When thou didst hate him worst, thou lov'dst him　　115
　　better
Than ever thou lov'dst Cassius.

**Brutus**

　　　　　　　　　　Sheathe your dagger:
Be angry when you will, it shall have scope;
Do what you will, dishonor shall be humor.
O Cassius, you are yoked with a lamb,　　120
That carries anger as the flint bears fire,
Who, much enforced, shows a hasty spark
And straight is cold again.

**Cassius**

　　　　　　　Hath Cassius liv'd
To be but mirth and laughter to his Brutus,　　125

133 **rash humor** Cassius was characterized by Plutarch as one who had "from his youth a natural hatred and rancor against the whole race of tyrants."

136 **over-earnest** perhaps, *overbearing.*

When grief and blood ill-temper'd vexeth him?
**Brutus**
When I spoke that, I was ill-temper'd too.
**Cassius**
Do you confess so much? Give me your hand.
**Brutus**
And my heart too.
**Cassius**
     O Brutus!                              130
**Brutus**
        What's the matter?
**Cassius**
Have not you love enough to bear with me,
When that rash humor which my mother gave me
Makes me forgetful?
**Brutus**
       Yes, Cassius, and from henceforth,   135
When you are over-earnest with your Brutus,
He'll think your mother chides, and leave you so.
**Poet**
[*Within*]   Let me go in to see the generals;
There is some grudge between 'em; 'tis not meet
They be alone.                                              140
**Lucilius**
[*Within*]   You shall not come to them.
**Poet**
[*Within*]   Nothing but death shall stay me.

 *Enter Poet, followed by Lucilius, Titinius, and
 Lucius.*

**Cassius**
How now! what's the matter?
**Poet**
For shame, you generals! what do you mean?
Love, and be friends, as two such men should be;   145
For I have seen more years, I'm sure, than ye.

151 **jigging**   rhyming badly, with a sing-song rhythm.

161–162 **Of your philosophy you make no use/If you give place
to accidental evils**   You make improper use of the Stoic
philosophy you profess if you are affected by every minor
misfortune.

*Cassius*
Ha, ha! how vilely doth this cynic rhyme!
*Brutus*
Get you hence, sirrah; saucy fellow, hence!
*Cassius*
Bear with him, Brutus; 'tis his fashion.
*Brutus*
I'll know his humor when he knows his time:                    150
What should the wars do with these jigging fools?
Companion, hence!
*Cassius*
                    Away, away, be gone!
                              [*Exit Poet.*

*Brutus*
Lucilius and Titinius, bid the commanders
Prepare to lodge their companies tonight.                      155
*Cassius*
And come yourselves, and bring Messala with you
Immediately to us.
                    [*Exeunt Lucilius and Titinius.*
*Brutus*
                    Lucius, a bowl of wine!
                              [*Exit Lucius.*

*Cassius*
I did not think you could have been so angry.
*Brutus*
O Cassius, I am sick of many griefs.                           160
*Cassius*
Of your philosophy you make no use,
If you give place to accidental evils.
*Brutus*
No man bears sorrow better: Portia is dead.
*Cassius*
Ha! Portia!

168 **upon** of.

173 **swallow'd fire** Plutarch reported " . . . determining to kill herself, (Portia) took hot, burning coals and cast them in her mouth, and kept her mouth so close that she choked herself."

*Brutus*
> She is dead.                                                            165

*Cassius*
> How 'scap'd I killing when I cross'd you so?
> O insupportable and touching loss!
> Upon what sickness?

*Brutus*
>                       Impatient of my absence,
> And grief that young Octavius with Mark Antony         170
> Have made themselves so strong: for with her death
> That tidings came: with this she fell distract,
> And, her attendants absent, swallow'd fire.

*Cassius*
> And died so?

*Brutus*
>                 Even so.                                                175

*Cassius*
>                       O ye immortal gods!

*Reenter Lucius, with wine and taper.*

*Brutus*
> Speak no more of her. Give me a bowl of wine.
> In this I bury all unkindness, Cassius.
>                                          [*Drinks.*

*Cassius*
> My heart is thirsty for that noble pledge.
> Fill, Lucius, till the wine o'erswell the cup;         180
> I cannot drink too much of Brutus' love.
>                                          [*Drinks.*

*Brutus*
> Come in, Titinius!
>                                     [*Exit Lucius.*

*Reenter Titinius, with Messala.*

>              Welcome, good Messala.

191 **bending**   directing.
192 **tenor**   trend.

194 **proscription**   order, usually one involving death, exile, etc.

205 **writ of her?**   Critics differ as to the reason for Brutus's de-
nial of knowledge of Portia's death which he previously
described to Cassius. Some suggest this scene represents a
combination of several stage scripts which were by mistake
combined. This might account for the inconsistency and the
seeming coldness of Brutus's "Why, farewell Portia."

Now sit we close about this taper here,
And call in question our necessities.                        185

**Cassius**
Portia, art thou gone?

**Brutus**
                    No more, I pray you.
Messala, I have here received letters,
That young Octavius and Mark Antony
Come down upon us with a mighty power,                        190
Bending their expedition toward Philippi.

**Messala**
Myself have letters of the self-same tenor.

**Brutus**
With what addition?

**Messala**
That by proscription and bills of outlawry
Octavius, Anthony, and Lepidus                                195
Have put to death an hundred senators.

**Brutus**
Therein our letters do not well agree;
Mine speak of seventy senators that died
By their proscriptions, Cicero being one.

**Cassius**
Cicero one!                                                  200

**Messala**
            Cicero is dead,
And by that order of proscription.
Had you your letters from your wife, my lord?

**Brutus**
No, Messala.

**Messala**
Nor nothing in your letters writ of her?                     205

**Brutus**
Nothing, Messala.

**Messala**
            That, methinks, is strange.

208 **aught** anything.

217 **art** theory.

219 **alive** Brutus means that he and Cassius, the living, have work to do from which the dead (like Portia) have been released.

230 **forc'd affection** are not really friendly.

*Brutus*

Why ask you? hear you aught of her in yours?

*Messala*

No, my lord.

*Brutus*

Now, as you are a Roman, tell me true.    210

*Messala*

Then like a Roman bear the truth I tell:

For certain she is dead, and by strange manner.

*Brutus*

Why, farewell, Portia. We must die, Messala:

With meditating that she must die once

I have the patience to endure it now.    215

*Messala*

Even so great men great losses should endure.

*Cassius*

I have as much of this in art as you,

But yet my nature could not bear it so.

*Brutus*

Well, to our work alive. What do you think

Of marching to Philippi presently?    220

*Cassius*

I do not think it good.

*Brutus*

                              Your reason?

*Cassius*

                                        This it is:

'Tis better that the enemy seek us:

So shall he waste his means, weary his soldiers,    225

Doing himself offense; whilst we lying still

Are full of rest, defense, and nimbleness.

*Brutus*

Good reasons must of force give place to better.

The people 'twixt Philippi and this ground

Do stand but in a forc'd affection,    230

239 **under your pardon**   by your leave.
240 **tried the utmost of our friends**   exploited to the fullest those who support us.

246 **omitted**   neglected.

249 **when it serves**   when it is available.

255 **niggard**   to attend to inadequately.

258 **hence**   go.

For they have grudg'd us contribution:
The enemy, marching along by them,
By them shall make a fuller number up,
Come on refresh'd, new-added, and encourag'd;
From which advantage shall we cut him off                235
If at Philippi we do face him there,
These people at our back.

*Cassius*

                      Hear me, good brother.

*Brutus*

Under your pardon. You must note beside
That we have tried the utmost of our friends,             240
Our legions are brim-full, our cause is ripe:
The enemy increaseth every day;
We, at the height, are ready to decline.
There is a tide in the affairs of men
Which taken at the flood leads on to fortune;             245
Omitted, all the voyage of their life
Is bound in shallows and in miseries.
On such a full sea are we now afloat,
And we must take the current when it serves,
Or lose our ventures.                                     250

*Cassius*

                Then, with your will, go on;
We'll along ourselves and meet them at Philippi.

*Brutus*

The deep of night is crept upon our talk,
And nature must obey necessity;
Which we will niggard with a little rest.                 255
There is no more to say?

*Cassius*

               No more. Good night:
Early tomorrow will we rise and hence.

*Brutus*

Lucius! [*Reenter Lucius.*] My gown. [*Exit Lucius.*]
    Farewell, good Messala:

271 **gown**   dressing gown.

274 **o'er-watch'd**   worn out from lack of sleep.

Good night, Titinius: noble, noble Cassius,                   260
Good night, and good repose.

*Cassius*

O my dear brother!
This was an ill beginning of the night:
Never come such division 'tween our souls!
Let it not, Brutus.                                          265

*Brutus*

Every thing is well.

*Cassius*

Good night, my lord.

*Brutus*

Good night, good brother.

*Titinius and Messala*

Good night, Lord Brutus.

*Brutus*

Farewell, every one.                   270
[*Exeunt all but Brutus.*

*Reenter Lucius, with the gown.*

Give me the gown. Where is thy instrument?

*Lucius*

Here in the tent.

*Brutus*

What, thou speak'st drowsily?
Poor knave, I blame thee not; thou art o'er-watch'd.
Call Claudius and some other of my men;                      275
I'll have them sleep on cushions in my tent.

*Lucius*

Varro and Claudius!

*Enter Varro and Claudius.*

*Varro*

Calls my lord?

*Brutus*

I pray you, sirs, lie in my tent and sleep;

282 **stand**  stay on watch.

284 **bethink me**  decide, consider.

302 **mace**  a weapon like a club.

It may be I shall raise you by and by                         280
On business to my brother Cassius.
*Varro*
So please you, we will stand and watch your pleasure.
*Brutus*
I will not have it so: lie down, good sirs;
It may be I shall otherwise bethink me.
Look, Lucius, here's the book I sought for so;          285
I put it in the pocket of my gown.
> [*Varro and Claudius lie down.*
*Lucius*
I was sure your lordship did not give it me.
*Brutus*
Bear with me, good boy, I am much forgetful.
Canst thou hold up thy heavy eyes awhile,
And touch thy instrument a strain or two?             290
*Lucius*
Aye, my lord, an 't please you.
*Brutus*
> It does, my boy:
I trouble thee too much, but thou art willing.
*Lucius*
It is my duty, sir.
*Brutus*
I should not urge thy duty past thy might;             295
I know young bloods look for a time of rest.
*Lucius*
I have slept, my lord, already.
*Brutus*
It was well done; and thou shalt sleep again.
I will not hold thee long: if I do live,
I will be good to thee.                                            300
> [*Music, and a song.*
This is a sleepy tune. O murd'rous slumber,
Lay'st thou thy leaden mace upon my boy,
That plays thee music? Gentle knave, good night;

314 **hair to stare**   hair to stand on end.

326 **false**   out of tune.

I will not do thee so much wrong to wake thee:
If thou dost nod, thou break'st thy instrument;     305
I'll take it from thee; and, good boy, good night.
Let me see, let me see; is not the leaf turn'd down
Where I left reading? Here it is, I think.

                              [*Sits down.*

   *Enter the Ghost of Cæsar.*

How ill this taper burns! Ha! who comes here?
I think it is the weakness of mine eyes     310
That shapes this monstrous apparition.
It comes upon me. Art thou any thing?
Art thou some god, some angel, or some devil,
That mak'st my blood cold, and my hair to stare?
Speak to me what thou art.     315

*Ghost*
Thy evil spirit, Brutus.

*Brutus*
                    Why com'st thou?

*Ghost*
To tell thee thou shalt see me at Philippi.

*Brutus*
Well; then I shall see thee again.

*Ghost*
Aye, at Philippi.     320

*Brutus*
Why, I will see thee at Philippi then.

                              [*Exit Ghost.*

Now I have taken heart thou vanishest.
Ill spirit, I would hold more talk with thee.
Boy, Lucius! Varro! Claudius! Sirs, awake!
Claudius!     325

*Lucius*
The strings, my lord, are false.

*Brutus*
He thinks he still is at his instrument.
Lucius, awake!

330 **criedst out** Brutus, according to some critics, is testing Lucius (as he later tests Messala and Varro) to find out if they have seen Cæsar's ghost.

343 **commend me** give my greetings.
344 **set on his pow'rs betimes before** move his troops forward earlier than originally planned.

*Lucius*
  My lord?
*Brutus*
  Didst thou dream, Lucius, that thou so criedst out?      330
*Lucius*
  My lord, I do not know that I did cry.

*Brutus*
  Yes, that thou didst: didst thou see any thing?
*Lucius*
  Nothing, my lord.
*Brutus*
  Sleep again, Lucius. Sirrah Claudius!
  [*To Varro*]    Fellow thou, awake!                       335
*Varro*
  My lord?
*Claudius*
  My lord?
*Brutus*
  Why did you so cry out, sirs, in your sleep?
*Varro and Claudius*
  Did we, my lord?
*Brutus*
                  Aye: saw you any thing?                    340
*Varro*
  No, my lord, I saw nothing.
*Claudius*
                  Nor I, my lord
*Brutus*
  Go and commend me to my brother Cassius;
  Bid him set on his pow'rs betimes before,
  And we will follow.                                        345
*Varro and Claudius*
                  It shall be done, my lord.
                                      [*Exeunt.*

7 **in their bosoms**   in their confidence.

17 **softly**   slowly.

# ACT V

*Enter Octavius, Antony, and their army.*

**Octavius**
Now, Antony, our hopes are answered:
You said the enemy would not come down,
But keep the hills and upper regions;
It proves not so: their battles are at hand;
They mean to warn us at Philippi here,      5
Answering before we do demand of them.

**Antony**
Tut, I am in their bosoms, and I know
Wherefore they do it: they could be content
To visit other places; and come down
With fearful bravery, thinking by this face      10
To fasten in our thoughts that they have courage;
But 'tis not so.

    *Enter a Messenger.*

**Messenger**
              Prepare you, generals:
The enemy comes on in gallant show;
Their bloody sign of battle is hung out,      15
And something to be done immediately.

**Antony**
Octavius, lead your battle softly on,
Upon the left hand of the even field.

**Octavius**
Upon the right hand I; keep thou the left.

20 **exigent**   crisis.

22 **parley**   talk.

36 **Hybla bees**   Mount Hybla in Sicily was famous for its honey.

Antony
  Why do you cross me in this exigent?                      20
Octavius
  I do not cross you; but I will do so.

                                          [March.

      Drum. Enter Brutus, Cassius, and their army;
      Lucilius, Titinius, Messala, and others.

Brutus
  They stand, and would have parley.
Cassius
  Stand fast, Titinius: we must out and talk.
Octavius
  Mark Antony, shall we give sign of battle?
Antony
  No, Cæsar, we will answer on their charge.               25
  Make forth; the generals would have some words.
Octavius
  Stir not until the signal.
Brutus
  Words before blows: is it so, countrymen?
Octavius
  Not that we love words better, as you do.
Brutus
  Good words are better than bad strokes, Octavius.        30
Antony
  In your bad strokes, Brutus, you give good words:
  Witness the hole you made in Cæsar's heart,
  Crying "Long live! hail, Cæsar!"
Cassius
                          Antony,
  The posture of your blows are yet unknown;               35
  But for your words, they rob the Hybla bees,
  And leave them honeyless.
Antony
                          Not stingless too.

52 **proof** the battle.

57 **another Cæsar** Octavius Cæsar.

66 **masker** one who takes part in masques, performances which combined music, dance, and masquerade.

*Brutus*

    O, yes, and soundless too;
    For you have stol'n their buzzing, Antony,                    40
    And very wisely threat before you sting.

*Antony*

    Villains, you did not so, when your vile daggers
    Hack'd one another in the sides of Cæsar:
    You show'd your teeth like apes, and fawn'd like
        hounds,
    And bow'd like bondmen, kissing Cæsar's feet;                    45
    Whilst damned Casca, like a cur, behind
    Struck Cæsar on the neck. O you flatterers!

*Cassius*

    Flatterers! Now, Brutus, thank yourself:
    This tongue had not offended so today,
    If Cassius might have rul'd.                    50

*Octavius*

    Come, come, the cause: if arguing make us sweat,
    The proof of it will turn to redder drops.
    Look,
    I draw a sword against conspirators;
    When think you that the sword goes up again?                    55
    Never, till Cæsar's three and thirty wounds
    Be well aveng'd, or till another Cæsar
    Have added slaughter to the sword of traitors.

*Brutus*

    Cæsar, thou canst not die by traitors' hands,
    Unless thou bring'st them with thee.                    60

*Octavius*

                    So I hope;
    I was not born to die on Brutus' sword.

*Brutus*

    O, if thou wert the noblest of thy strain,
    Young man, thou couldst not die more honorable.

*Cassius*

    A peevish schoolboy, worthless of such honor,                    65
    Join'd with a masker and a reveler!

71 **stomachs** courage.

90 **consorted** accompanied.

Antony

　　Old Cassius still!

Octavius

　　　　　　　　Come, Antony; away!

　　Defiance, traitors, hurl we in your teeth;

　　If you dare fight today, come to the field:　　　　70

　　If not, when you have stomachs.

　　　　　　　[*Exeunt Octavius, Antony, and their army.*

Cassius

　　Why, now, blow wind, swell billow, and swim bark!

　　The storm is up, and all is on the hazard.

Brutus

　　Ho, Lucilius! hark, a word with you.

Lucilius

　　　　　　　[*Standing forth*]　My lord?　　　　75

　　　　　　　[*Brutus and Lucilius converse apart.*

Cassius

　　Messala!

Messala

　　[*Standing forth*]　What says my general?

Cassius

　　　　　　　　　　　　　Messala,

　　This is my birthday; as this very day

　　Was Cassius born. Give me thy hand, Messala:　　80

　　Be thou my witness that, against my will,

　　As Pompey was, am I compell'd to set

　　Upon one battle all our liberties.

　　You know that I held Epicurus strong,

　　And his opinion: now I change my mind　　　　85

　　And partly credit things that do presage.

　　Coming from Sardis, on our former ensign

　　Two mighty eagles fell, and there they perch'd,

　　Gorging and feeding from our soldiers' hands;

　　Who to Philippi here consorted us:　　　　90

　　This morning are they fled away and gone;

　　And in their steads do ravens, crows, and kites

111 **Cato**   Brutus's father-in-law.

115 **The time of life**   the natural or ordained end of life.
116 **stay**   wait for.

120 **Thorough**   through.

Fly o'er our heads and downward look on us,
As we were sickly prey: their shadows seem
A canopy most fatal, under which                          95
Our army lies, ready to give up the ghost.

*Messala*

Believe not so.

*Cassius*

                    I but believe it partly,
For I am fresh of spirit and resolved
To meet all perils very constantly.                       100

*Brutus*

Even so, Lucilius.

*Cassius*

                    Now, most noble Brutus,
The gods today stand friendly, that we may,
Lovers in peace, lead on our days to age!
But, since the affairs of men rest still incertain,       105
Let's reason with the worst that may befall.
If we do lose this battle, then is this
The very last time we shall speak together:
What are you then determined to do?

*Brutus*

Even by the rule of that philosophy                       110
By which I did blame Cato for the death
Which he did give himself: I know not how,
But I do find it cowardly and vile,
For fear of what might fall, so to prevent
The time of life: arming myself with patience             115
To stay the providence of some high powers
That govern us below.

*Cassius*

                    Then, if we lose this battle,
You are contented to be led in triumph
Thorough the streets of Rome?                             120

*Brutus*

No, Cassius, no: think not, thou noble Roman,

Stage directions **Alarum**   a trumpet call to arms.

1 **bills**   notes, messages.
2 **other side**   Cassius' wing of the army.

That ever Brutus will go bound to Rome;
He bears too great a mind. But this same day
Must end that work the ides of March begun;
And whether we shall meet again I know not.                    125
Therefore our everlasting farewell take.
For ever, and for ever, farewell, Cassius!
If we do meet again, why, we shall smile;
If not, why then this parting was well made.

Cassius

For ever and for ever farewell, Brutus!                        130
If we do meet again, we'll smile indeed;
If not, 'tis true this parting was well made.

Brutus

Why then, lead on. O, that a man might know
The end of this day's business ere it come!
But it sufficeth that the day will end,                        135
And then the end is known. Come, ho! away!

                                            [*Exeunt.*

## Scene 2. *The field of battle*

*Alarum. Enter Brutus and Messala.*

Brutus

Ride, ride, Messala, ride, and give these bills
Unto the legions on the other side:

                                    [*Loud  alarum.*

Let them set on at once; for I perceive
But cold demeanor in Octavius' wing,
And sudden push gives them the overthrow.                      5
Ride, ride, Messala: let them all come down.

                                            [*Exeunt.*

1 **villains**   his own men.

3 **ensign**   both the flag and its bearer.

16 **hide thy spurs**   dig your spurs deeply.

## Scene 3. *Another part of the field*

*Alarums. Enter Cassius and Titinius.*

*Cassius*

O, look, Titinius, look, the villains fly!
Myself have to mine own turn'd enemy:
This ensign here of mine was turning back;
I slew the coward, and did take it from him.

*Titinius*

O Cassius, Brutus gave the word too early;                    5
Who, having some advantage on Octavius,
Took it too eagerly: his soldiers fell to spoil,
Whilst we by Antony are all enclos'd.

*Enter Pindarus.*

*Pindarus*

Fly further off, my lord, fly further off;
Mark Antony is in your tents, my lord:                       10
Fly, therefore, noble Cassius, fly far off.

*Cassius*

This hill is far enough. Look, look, Titinius;
Are those my tents where I perceive the fire?

*Titinius*

They are, my lord.

*Cassius*

                    Titinius, if thou lovest me,              15
Mount thou my horse and hide thy spurs in him,
Till he have brought thee up to yonder troops
And here again; that I may rest assur'd
Whether yond troops are friend or enemy.

*Titinius*

I will be here again, even with a thought.                   20

[*Exit.*

26 **compass**   full circle.

32 **light**   get down from his horse.

44 **hilts**   the plural form was common in Shakespeare's time.

Cassius
> Go, Pindarus, get higher on that hill;
> My sight was ever thick; regard Titinius,
> And tell me what thou notest about the field.
> > [*Pindarus ascends the hill.*
> This day I breathed first: time is come round,
> And where I did begin, there shall I end;                    25
> My life is run his compass. Sirrah, what news?

Pindarus
> [*Above*]   O my lord!

Cassius
> What news?

Pindarus
> [*Above*]   Titinius is enclosed round about
> With horsemen, that make to him on the spur;                 30
> Yet he spurs on. Now they are almost on him.
> Now, Titinius! Now some light. O, he lights too.
> He's ta'en. [*Shout.*] And, hark! they shout for joy.

Cassius
> Come down; behold no more.
> O, coward that I am, to live so long,                        35
> To see my best friend ta'en before my face!

> > *Pindarus descends.*

> Come hither, sirrah:
> In Parthia did I take thee prisoner;
> And then I swore thee, saving of thy life,
> That whatsoever I did bid thee do,                           40
> Thou shouldst attempt it. Come now, keep thine oath;
> Now be a freeman; and with this good sword,
> That ran through Cæsar's bowels, search this bosom.
> Stand not to answer: here, take thou the hilts;
> And when my face is cover'd, as 'tis now,                    45
> Guide thou the sword.
> > > [*Pindarus stabs him.*
> > > Cæsar, thou art reveng'd,

53 **change**   exchange of fortune.
54 **power**   army.

67 **The sun of Rome**   the glory of Rome.

Even with the sword that kill'd thee.

> [*Dies.*

**Pindarus**

So, I am free; yet would not so have been,
Durst I have done my will. O Cassius!                          50
Far from this country Pindarus shall run,
Where never Roman shall take note of him.

> [*Exit.*

*Reenter Titinius with Messala.*

**Messala**

It is but change, Titinius; for Octavius
Is overthrown by noble Brutus' power,
As Cassius' legions are by Antony.                            55

**Titinius**

These tidings will well comfort Cassius.

**Messala**

Where did you leave him?

**Titinius**

                              All disconsolate,
With Pindarus his bondman, on this hill.

**Messala**

Is not that he that lies upon the ground?                     60

**Titinius**

He lies not like the living. O my heart!

**Messala**

Is not that he?

**Titinius**

                    No, this was he, Messala,
But Cassius is no more. O setting sun,
As in thy red rays thou dost sink to night,                   65
So in his red blood Cassius' day is set,
The sun of Rome is set! Our day is gone;
Clouds, dews, and dangers come; our deeds are done!
Mistrust of my success hath done this deed.

72 **apt**   ready.

90 **hold**   wait.

92 **apace**   quickly.

Messala

Mistrust of good success hath done this deed.      70
O hateful error, melancholy's child,
Why dost thou show to the apt thoughts of men
The things that are not? O error, soon conceiv'd,
Thou never com'st unto a happy birth,
But kill'st the mother that engender'd thee!      75

Titinius

What, Pindarus! where art thou, Pindarus?

Messala

Seek him, Titinius, whilst I go to meet
The noble Brutus, thrusting this report
Into his ears: I may say "thrusting" it,
For piercing steel and darts envenomed      80
Shall be as welcome to the ears of Brutus
As tidings of this sight.

Titinius

                    Hie you, Messala,
And I will seek for Pindarus the while.

                              [Exit Messala.

Why didst thou send me forth, brave Cassius?      85
Did I not meet thy friends? and did not they
Put on my brows this wreath of victory,
And bid me give it thee? Didst thou not hear their
    shouts?
Alas, thou hast misconstrued every thing!
But, hold thee, take this garland on thy brow;      90
Thy Brutus bid me give it thee, and I
Will do his bidding. Brutus, come apace,
And see how I regarded Caius Cassius.
By your leave, gods: this is a Roman's part.
Come, Cassius' sword, and find Titinius' heart.      95

                              [Kills himself.


Alarum. Reenter Messala, with Brutus, young Cato,
and others.

102 **proper**   personal (used for greater emphasis).

108 **fellow**   match, equal.

*Brutus*

Where, where, Messala, doth his body lie?

*Messala*

Lo, yonder, and Titinius mourning it.

*Brutus*

Titinius' face is upward.

*Cato*

He is slain.

*Brutus*

O Julius Cæsar, thou are mighty yet!          100
Thy spirit walks abroad, and turns our swords
In our own proper entrails.

[*Low alarums.*

*Cato*

Brave Titinius!
Look, whether he have not crown'd dead Cassius!

*Brutus*

Are yet two Romans living such as these?          105
The last of all the Romans, fare thee well!
It is impossible that ever Rome
Should breed thy fellow. Friends, I owe moe tears
To this dead man than you shall see me pay.
I shall find time, Cassius, I shall find time.          110
Come therefore, and to Thasos send his body:
His funerals shall not be in our camp,
Lest it discomfort us. Lucilius, come,
And come, young Cato: let us to the field.
Labeo and Flavius, set our battles on.          115
'Tis three o'clock; and, Romans, yet ere night
We shall try fortune in a second fight.

[*Exeunt.*

2 **What bastard . . . ?** Who is of such base blood that he does not hold his head up?

14 **so much** Some editors assume that Lucilius offers money. Most believe that the capture of Brutus is of such strategic and psychological importance that no money is intended in these words.

## Scene 4. Another part of the field

*Alarum. Enter, fighting, Soldiers of both armies;*
*then Brutus, young Cato, Lucilius, and others.*

**Brutus**
Yet, countrymen, O, yet hold up your heads!
**Cato**
What bastard doth not? Who will go with me?
I will proclaim my name about the field.
I am the son of Marcus Cato, ho!
A foe to tyrants, and my country's friend;                    5
I am the son of Marcus Cato, ho!
**Brutus**
And I am Brutus, Marcus Brutus, I;
Brutus, my country's friend; know me for Brutus!
                                                    [*Exit.*

**Lucilius**
O young and noble Cato, art thou down?
Why, now thou diest as bravely as Titinius,                   10
And mayst be honor'd, being Cato's son.
**First Soldier**
Yield, or thou diest.
**Lucilius**
                        Only I yield to die:
    [*Offering money*
There is so much that thou wilt kill me straight;
Kill Brutus, and be honor'd in his death.                     15
**First Soldier**
We must not. A noble prisoner!
**Second Soldier**
Room, ho! Tell Antony, Brutus is ta'en.
**First Soldier**
I'll tell the news. Here comes the general.

19 **ta'en**   taken.

33 **chanc'd**   has worked out.

*Enter Antony.*

Brutus is ta'en, Brutus is ta'en, my lord.

**Antony**

Where is he?                                                             20

**Lucilius**

Safe, Antony; Brutus is safe enough:
I dare assure thee that no enemy
Shall ever take alive the noble Brutus:
The gods defend him from so great a shame!
When you do find him, or alive or dead,                                  25
He will be found like Brutus, like himself.

**Antony**

This is not Brutus, friend, but, I assure you,
A prize no less in worth: keep this man safe,
Give him all kindness: I had rather have
Such men my friends than enemies. Go on,                                 30
And see whether Brutus be alive or dead,
And bring us word unto Octavius' tent
How every thing is chanc'd.

                                        [*Exeunt.*


## Scene 5. *Another part of the field*

*Enter Brutus, Dardanius, Clitus, Strato, and
Volumnius.*


**Brutus**

Come, poor remains of friends, rest on this rock.

**Clitus**

Statilius show'd the torch-light, but, my lord,
He came not back: he is or ta'en or slain.

**5 deed in fashion** Brutus refers here to the deaths of Cassius, Titinius, etc.

**17 list** listen to.

**Brutus**

Sit thee down, Clitus: slaying is the word;
It is a deed in fashion. Hark thee, Clitus.          5

*[Whispering.*

**Clitus**

What, I, my lord? No, not for all the world.

**Brutus**

Peace then, no words.

**Clitus**

I'll rather kill myself.

**Brutus**

Hark thee, Dardanius.

*[Whispering.*

**Dardanius**

Shall I do such a deed?          10

**Clitus**

O Dardanius!

**Dardanius**

O Clitus!

**Clitus**

What ill request did Brutus make to thee?

**Dardanius**

To kill him, Clitus. Look, he meditates.

**Clitus**

Now is that noble vessel full of grief,          15
That it runs over even at his eyes.

**Brutus**

Come hither, good Volumnius; list a word.

**Volumnius**

What says my lord?

**Brutus**

Why, this, Volumnius:
The ghost of Cæsar hath appear'd to me          20
Two several times by night; at Sardis once,

27 **pit**  trap for wild animals or grave for men, or final abyss.

42 **vile conquest**  Even in death Brutus clings to the belief that the death of Cæsar was necessary.

And this last night here in Philippi fields:
I know my hour is come.

*Volumnius*

                    Not so, my lord.

*Brutus*

Nay, I am sure it is, Volumnius.                          25
Thou seest the world, Volumnius, how it goes;
Our enemies have beat us to the pit:

                              [*Low alarums.*

It is more worthy to leap in ourselves
Than tarry till they push us. Good Volumnius,
Thou know'st that we two went to school together:      30
Even for that our love of old, I prithee,
Hold thou my sword-hilts, whilst I run on it.

*Volumnius*

That's not an office for a friend, my lord.

                              [*Alarum still.*

*Clitus*

Fly, fly, my lord; there is no tarrying here.

*Brutus*

Farewell to you; and you; and you, Volumnius.          35
Strato, thou hast been all this while asleep;
Farewell to thee too, Strato. Countrymen,
My heart doth joy that yet in all my life
I found no man but he was true to me.
I shall have glory by this losing day,                  40
More than Octavius and Mark Antony
By this vile conquest shall attain unto.
So, fare you well at once; for Brutus' tongue
Hath almost ended his life's history:
Night hangs upon mine eyes; my bones would rest,       45
That have but labor'd to attain this hour.

              [*Alarum. Cry within, "Fly, fly, fly!"*

*Clitus*

Fly, my lord, fly.

**51 smatch**   taste, bit.

**66 entertain**   hire, employ.

**68 prefer**   refer, recommend.

Brutus

Hence! I will follow.
[Exeunt Clitus, Dardanius, and Volumnius.
I prithee, Strato, stay thou by thy lord:
Thou art a fellow of a good respect;                         50
Thy life hath had some smatch of honor in it:
Hold then my sword, and turn away thy face,
While I do run upon it. Wilt thou, Strato?

Strato

Give me your hand first: fare you well, my lord.

Brutus

Farewell, good Strato.                                       55
[Runs on his sword.
Cæsar, now be still.
I kill'd not thee with half so good a will.
[Dies.

Alarum. Retreat. Enter Octavius, Antony, Messala,
Lucilius, and the army.

Octavius

What man is that?

Messala

My master's man. Strato, where is thy master?

Strato

Free from the bondage you are in, Messala:                  60
The conquerors can but make a fire of him;
For Brutus only overcame himself,
And no man else hath honor by his death.

ucilius

So Brutus should be found. I thank thee, Brutus,
That thou hast prov'd Lucilius' saying true.                 65

Octavius

All that serv'd Brutus, I will entertain them.
Fellow, wilt thou bestow thy time with me?

Strato

Aye, if Messala will prefer me to you.

85 **order'd**   handled, treated.

87 **part**   share.

*Octavius*

Do so, good Messala.

*Messala*

How died my master, Strato?                                   70

*Strato*

I held the sword, and he did run on it.

*Messala*

Octavius, then take him to follow thee,
That did the latest service to my master.

*Antony*

This was the noblest Roman of them all:
All the conspirators, save only he,                           75
Did that they did in envy of great Cæsar;
He only, in a general honest thought
And common good to all, made one of them.
His life was gentle, and the elements
So mix'd in him that Nature might stand up                    80
And say to all the world "This was a man!"

*Octavius*

According to his virtue let us use him,
With all respect and rites of burial.
Within my tent his bones tonight shall lie
Most like a soldier, order'd honorably.                       85
So call the field to rest, and let's away,
To part the glories of this happy day.

                                        [*Exeunt.*

# READER'S GUIDE

*Helene  Cunningham*

*Formerly Teacher of English*
*Newtown High School, New York City*

# INTRODUCTION

Shakespeare's *Julius Cæsar* was written and first performed almost four hundred years ago. Since then, audiences and readers have been held in suspense by the story, fascinated with the characters, stirred by the lines, thrilled with the spectacle of its dramatic scenes. Moreover, you will find, as others have, that this play has another quality, which it shares with all great masterpieces. Although it was written in 1599, and tells of people who lived two thousand years ago, it speaks to each of us today as members of our own society, faced with the personal and public problems of our own times. Thus, *Julius Cæsar* has an undying and universal quality in two ways: as a work of dramatic literature and as an interpretation of human experience. Shakespeare himself foresaw and expressed this quality in these prophetic lines from the play:

> How many ages hence
> Shall this our lofty scene be acted over
> In states unborn and accents yet unknown!

It will be helpful to you to note at the outset that a Shakespearean play is a somewhat different kind of reading experience from those you may be more accustomed to. A play is written to be performed on the stage. When it is read from the printed page, the reader must use skill and imagination to transform the dialogue into the living action of the stage. He must visualize the appearance, manner, and acts of the characters who speak the lines and the scene in which the action occurs. In the case of Shakespeare, specifically, the language is that of Elizabethan times and, for the most part, that of poetry. Too, it is a language written with the supreme skill of the greatest writer who ever lived. For all of these reasons, you will need to bring a special kind of attention and interpretation to your reading of this play.

The purpose of this *Reader's Guide* is to help you to understand and enjoy *Julius Cæsar*. To achieve that purpose, you will be asked to work with questions and to do exercises around these five main topics:

1. Following the Story
2. Studying the Characters
3. Visualizing the Acting and Staging
4. Understanding and Appreciating the Lines
5. Exploring Issues of Importance in Human Experience

Before beginning your reading of *Julius Cæsar* and dealing with the *Reader's Guide* problems, you will find it helpful to study the following explanatory comments on these five topics.

## FOLLOWING THE STORY

In reading the play, you will want, first, to be sure that you follow the story and appreciate the skill with which the story line, or plot, has been developed. You will want to know *what* happens and foresee what is likely to happen. You will want to understand the *how* and the *why* of the course of events. The essential ingredient of a dramatic plot is **conflict**. We all have goals, immediate or distant, significant or trivial. In our attempts to achieve them we are often opposed—by another person or persons; by the society or community in which we live; by elements of nature; even, most importantly, by conflicting impulses and needs within ourselves. While real-life conflicts are often difficult and unpleasant, we actually enjoy fictional conflicts. One reason is that we do not have to resolve them. Someone else does it for us. The other reason is that we develop a better understanding of the conflicts we face in our own lives through an understanding of fictional conflicts.

The second important ingredient of a dramatic plot is **suspense**. Although we often caution a friend, "Don't keep me in suspense," we never say this to an author. The tension and anxiety which is painful in real life becomes pleasurable excitement as we follow a suspenseful movie or play.

In the development of conflict and the handling of suspense, the playwright is helped by five principles of dramatic construction developed thousands of years ago by the great Greek dramatists:

**1. The introduction, or exposition.** This portion sets the scene, introduces the characters, creates the atmosphere, and indicates the conflicts. Most importantly, it creates for the main character (who in a drama is called the **protagonist**) an incident which causes him or her to consider action against the opposing force or forces.

**2. The rising action.** The incident which first made the protagonist recognize the need for action is followed by other incidents which make collision between the opposing forces more and more likely. These incidents alternately favor one side or the other (predominantly the side of the protagonist) and finally make confrontation inevitable.

**3. The climax.** The protagonist acts in some significant way, hoping to end the conflict. This is usually the most stirring moment of the play. Although it rouses our emotions, we are immediately made aware that it has not disposed of the conflict.

**4. The consequences.** Attention is now directed to the results of the climax. Now we see that the climax was really also the turning point of the play in terms of the protagonist's fortunes, and begin to realize that success or failure will follow. Suspense, however, continues as incidents of alternate success or failure (predominantly of failure if the play is a tragedy) keep us in doubt as to the outcome.

**5. The outcome.** This is, of course, the ending. When it comes we must be satisfied that it is the natural and logical result of all the earlier events of the story.

What use can you make in following the plot of *Julius Cæsar* of what you now know about the basic ingredients and the method of construction of a dramatic plot? *Julius Cæsar* consists of five acts. These acts conform generally in purpose and development to the five movements of dramatic construction. You can, therefore, find the inciting incident, trace the complicating action to its climax, decide what is the probable outcome, follow the seesaw circumstances of the resolution of the conflict, pinpoint the moment of final suspense, and contemplate the outcome. The questions and exercises on FOLLOWING THE STORY in this *Guide* will help you to follow these developments.


## STUDYING THE CHARACTERS

Think about some of the people you have met in your life. In the beginning they were strangers. Then, your first impressions of these strangers were gradually formed, on the basis of their appearance, actions, and words—and, of course, their relations with and reactions to you. Sometimes, also, what other people said about a person may have strongly influenced your opinion. These impressions may not have been completely accurate or lasting. They were certainly added to, reevaluated, and refined as you got to know the individuals better. Gradually, by observing what they said and did, you built an image of what these people in particular and of what people in general were like. You recognized such abstract human emotions and motivations as *ambition, anger, courage, compassion, jealousy, pride, greed,* and *love.* Out of this observation and analysis also came, in part, the decision as to what you considered good and evil, fair and unfair, wise and foolish, weak and strong.

The study of the personality and conduct of characters in fiction is a conscious effort to apply the same techniques that we use instinctively in the effort to understand real people. In *Julius Cæsar,* the main characters are great historical figures, but they are also men and women. Shakespeare breathed life into these people, created their characters so effectively that Cæsar, Brutus, Cassius, and Mark Antony have become flesh and blood. As you read or listen to or visualize the play, look for the words and actions that are the clues to understanding the people in it —and through them, to understanding better yourself and the world you live in.


## VISUALIZING THE ACTING AND STAGING

One of the difficulties in reading a play is that it is meant to be acted on a stage before an audience. In addition to words, a play employs movement, expression, interpretation, spectacle, stage effects, costumes, and furnishings. It also implies an audience which, in effect, becomes a participant in the drama. How, then, can you simply read this play and enjoy the total effect which was meant to be achieved by its stage presentation?

Part of the answer is that you will not simply *read* this play. You will hear the lines spoken by people who know the play well and have learned to bring its characters, events, and spectacles to life for you. Your teacher will read aloud significant speeches and important scenes. At some time during your study of the play, you may have an opportunity to see films or hear recordings of professional performances of *Julius Cæsar*. You may, in addition, have an opportunity to see a production of this or some other Shakespearean play.

## Stage Directions

While the stage directions are few, they are significant. Note, for instance, the directions preceding the first entrance of the principal characters in Act I, Scene 2:

*Flourish. Enter Cæsar; Antony, for the course; Calpurnia, Portia, Decius, Cicero, Brutus, Cassius, and Casca; a great crowd following, among them a Soothsayer.*

A flourish is a trumpet fanfare which will call the audience's attention to the entrance of an important person. That important person is Cæsar. While the playwright gives no instructions as to how Cæsar enters, most productions have him carried in by servants, seated on a litter or kind of portable chair which would place him above the heads of the others. Walking next to the litter or immediately after it is Antony, who is dressed for the race he is going to run later in the scene. The wives of Cæsar and Brutus along with other important persons of the play come next. The crowd follows them, possibly at a little distance. Conspicuous in the crowd is a Soothsayer (fortune teller), who by his dress and manner undoubtedly stands out in that crowd as he does in the author's directions.

More important than the actual stage directions, of course, is the knowledge which a director has of the characters and future actions of the people who appear in this scene. You do not have this knowledge as you begin the play, but later, when you have met the characters, you can go back and imagine the way each might walk, the byplay that might go on in the crowd, and the differences in clothes and behavior which would distinguish the various characters in this scene.

There are other ways in which the playwright indicates action. When Cassius says, on hearing that Cæsar will be crowned, "I know where I will wear my dagger then; Cassius from bondage will deliver Cassius," we have an idea of the gesture which must accompany those words. Similarly, when Brutus points out to Cassius the angry spot that glows on Cæsar's brow and the way all who accompany him skulk like scolded children, we have a feeling how a director should present that scene

## The Soliloquy

How can a playwright express the thoughts of a character if the audience hears only the conversation of that character with other people? Shakespeare used the **soliloquy** (a speech by one character, alone on the stage, in which that person expresses his inner feelings, thoughts, and intentions). If this seems strange to you, remember that everything about a play, even its name, requires pretending. If you can pretend that a stage is a street in Rome, that an actor is Julius Cæsar, that people on the stage love or hate each other, it is easy to believe that the soliloquy is actually a glimpse into the mind of the character who delivers it.

## The Shakespearean Stage

The stage for which Shakespeare wrote was not the "picture frame" we know today. There were no footlights (in fact, all plays were acted in the afternoon, by natural light); no elaborate sets to indicate shifts of scene; no side wings into which actors could disappear or from which they could reappear; not even a curtain to pull down at the end of acts or scenes.

The stage was simply a wooden platform that jutted out into the middle of the section occupied by the audience and was partly covered by a small roof. At the rear of the platform was a curtained area which served as an inner room or for any intimate scene in which few characters were involved. At the back, two doors led to the dressing rooms of the actors and served for exit and entrance. There was also a balcony above the inner room and possibly balconies on the sides of the stage which, on occasion, may have seated important members of the audience. We say "possibly" and "perhaps" because, while we have engravings and other evidence of the theaters in which Shakespeare was first performed, the wooden buildings themselves long ago burned or were torn down. The actual stage "properties," by which we mean movable scenery and personal objects, must have been few. An armchair was a throne; boards on trestles made a banquet table; individual items like rugs or hangings or wreaths or scrolls or goblets or daggers were probably real.

As for the costumes, we have no evidence that *Julius Cæsar* or any other of Shakespeare's historical plays was acted in Shakespeare's time in the costume appropriate to its period. Cæsar enters at one point in a nightgown (dressing gown); Cassius tells Brutus to pluck Casca by the sleeve (we know that Roman togas had no sleeves). People in the play refer occasionally to the doublet, a jacket of the sixteenth and seventeenth centuries, which was unknown in Cæsar's time. Most scholars who have studied the play agree that some combination of contemporary (that is, Elizabethan) and Roman costume was worn by Shakespeare's actors. Possibly, as woodcuts of the period indicate, the men in the army scenes were dressed in breastplate armor (similar to the Roman armor) over Shakespearean doublets. They also probably wore Roman helmets and carried battle-axes and swords.

*Julius Cæsar* has been enacted in modern dress, in uniforms such as Mussolini and his army wore, and in authentic Roman dress. If Shakespeare's characters do not seem to be dressed always like ancient Romans, it is another proof of the timeless quality of the play.


## UNDERSTANDING AND APPRECIATING THE LINES

### Figurative Language

Here are four lines from the first act of *Julius Cæsar*. Cassius says to Brutus about Cæsar:

Why, man, he doth bestride the narrow world
Like a Colossus, and we petty men
Walk under his huge legs and peep about
To find ourselves dishonorable graves.

In these lines Cæsar is compared, imaginatively, to a giant whose legs straddle the world. Tiny men walk under him and peer fearfully up at the huge legs. Through this word picture, or image, the idea of Cæsar's power is represented vividly and forcefully.

The words used in this kind of imaginative comparison are called **figurative** because their meaning is not intended to be taken literally or directly. An idea or feeling is expressed or represented indirectly through the vivid image. There are two kinds of such imaginative comparison. A **simile** contains the words "like" or "as" to show that a comparison is being made. The passage quoted above is a simile, for Cæsar is said to bestride the world *like* a Colossus. In a **metaphor** the comparing words "like" and "as" do not appear. For example, the passage quoted above would become a metaphor if the lines read: "Why, man, he is a Colossus and doth bestride the narrow world, and we petty men. . . ." It is, of course, important both for understanding and appreciation to recognize that the words expressing the image in a metaphor are not to be read literally but are to be understood as representing a feeling or idea through a picture.

As you do the exercises in the *Guide*, your attention will be called to examples of simile, metaphor, and other types of figurative language for your greater enjoyment of this play.

### Special Meanings and Forms

Understanding the lines in a play by Shakespeare is not like making a fumbling translation of a foreign language. Shakespeare wrote early Modern English. This means that although he still used *thou*, *thee*, and *thine*, for example, he also used the modern *you*. When he asked a question, he said, "What, know you not?" instead of "What, don't you know?" Or, "And after that came he away?" whereas we would say, "And after that did he come away?" Some of his contractions (*'tis* and *i'*) may be unfamiliar to you, as well as his epithets (*Ho! Ye gods!*) which we, today, more often employ for humorous than serious effect. More difficult, perhaps, is the fact that sometimes, but not too often, the sense of a word used by Shakespeare is somewhat different from its modern meaning, or that a few of the words he used are now obsolete. For this reason, the explanation of difficult or unusual words or expressions is given on the same page so that you can, without inconvenience, locate quickly the meaning of the obsolete word or special Shakespearean expression.

## The Poetry of Shakespeare

Let us return, for a moment, to the quotation with which this section began. The lines are poetry. You could, however, write this sentence as prose if you wished.

Why, man, he doth bestride the narrow world like a Colossus, and we petty men walk under his huge legs and peep about to find ourselves dishonorable graves.

It still, you will agree, says the same thing. The sacrifice is not in sense, but to the eye and ear to which poetry appeals. The words are written in blank verse, which is unrhymed **iambic pentameter**, a beat particularly well suited to the English language and to the significant ideas Shakespeare's characters expressed in this and other plays. Iambic pentameter consists of *one unaccented beat followed by an accented beat, in a line of five metric feet.*

$$\breve{~}~/~~\breve{~}~/~~\breve{~}~/~~\breve{~}~/~~\breve{~}~/$$
$$\text{Why, man, | he doth | bestride | the nar | row world}$$
$$\quad 1 \qquad\quad 2 \qquad\quad 3 \qquad\quad 4 \qquad\quad 5$$

Note that generally the words significant to the sense or emotion of the line are accented and that less important words or syllables are usually unaccented. Listen, also, to the triumphant progression of the rhythm so well suited, in this case, to a play in which so many of the characters are famous orators. Shakespeare sometimes rhymed his lines, particularly at the end of a scene or to emphasize important incidents. He used prose for the speech of the common people, for letters, and when some important information had to be given quickly and clearly.

## EXPLORING ISSUES OF IMPORTANCE IN HUMAN EXPERIENCE

One of the most important contributions of the English-speaking world's greatest playwright and finest poet is his exploration of universal themes and his understanding of those aspects of human nature which do not change.

The themes and comments on human experience in *Julius Cæsar* relate to questions which trouble us today:

> Is violence an effective answer to violence?
>
> Should loyalty to a friend be more important than loyalty to the good of your community or loyalty to your own beliefs and ideals?
>
> Is murder ever justified?
>
> Can a man of principle and honor be a successful politician?
>
> Are people's decisions determined by logic or emotions?
>
> Do we ever really understand ourselves—or other people?

Some readers of *Julius Cæsar* have said that Shakespeare gave no answers to these questions, only extremely interesting illustrations of the questions themselves. Read the play and see what you think.

# QUESTIONS

## Act I, Scene 1

### FOLLOWING THE STORY

**1.** Why do the tribunes Flavius and Marullus rebuke the commoners?

**2.** Who was Pompey? What was the outcome of his conflict with Cæsar? (lines 36–51)

**3.** Which classes of Roman society are represented? How does each regard Cæsar?

**4.** Why does Marullus consider Cæsar's latest conquest no victory? Why does Flavius fear Cæsar? (lines 32–34; 72–75)

### STUDYING THE CHARACTERS

**5.** An important "character," the crowd, is introduced. How are you made to realize its fickle and thoughtless nature?

**6.** In what way does Flavius himself show disrespect for the gods? (lines 64–65)

### VISUALIZING THE ACTING AND STAGING

**7.** Below are stage directions the playwright might have given. At which point in the scene would you insert each?
   a. Members of the crowd push and shove each other.
   b. The crowd laughs.
   c. The speaker pulls one of the crowd to the center of the stage.
   d. Members of the crowd look guiltily at each other.
   e. The crowd goes out silently, by ones and twos.

**8.** What gesture might accompany each of the following statements? Make your selection from the suggestions offered below the statements.

a. "Hence! home, you idle creatures, get you home." (line 1)

b. "What trade, thou knave? thou naughty knave, what trade?" (line 15)

c. "You blocks, you stones, you worse than senseless things!" (line 35)

d. "To towers and windows, yea, to chimney-tops." (line 39)

    (1) Clenched fists raised in the air.

    (2) Gradual raising of the hand.

    (3) Imperious wave of the hand.

    (4) Shaking the person by the shoulder.

## UNDERSTANDING AND APPRECIATING THE LINES

**9.** This scene has an elaborate series of puns with which the cobbler delights the crowd and annoys the tribunes. List all the puns you can find with their two different meanings and spellings.

**10.** Explain the personification used in reference to the Tiber River. (lines 45–47)

**11.** The metaphor used by Flavius (lines 72–75) depends to a certain extent on a knowledge of falconry. The theory was that plucking feathers from the wings of a falcon would force it to fly at a height at which it could be seen and watched. With this understanding, express in your own words Flavius's meaning.

## EXPLORING ISSUES OF IMPORTANCE IN HUMAN EXPERIENCE

**12.** We talk of "mob psychology." In what ways are the words and manner of the cobbler different with the crowd around him than they might have been if he had met the tribunes when he was alone? Why does being part of a crowd or mob change the behavior of the individuals in it?

**13.** One of the most important observations on the behavior of people that you will find in this play is the tendency of some to bend, or "fashion," others to their own conclusions or purposes. What illustration of this do you find in Scene 1?

# Act I, Scene 2

## FOLLOWING THE STORY

**1.** What note of warning is sounded near the beginning of this scene?

**2.** What remarks by Brutus encourage Cassius to talk to him more openly about the conspiracy?

**3.** In many respects, the beginning of the conversation between Cassius and Brutus (lines 29–87) is a verbal duel.

    *a.* Who makes the first move? Why?

    *b.* Of what does Cassius complain? (lines 36-40) How does Brutus answer?

    *c.* Which lines first reveal Cassius' real intention? What is Brutus's reply?

    *d.* At which point does Cassius use Brutus's own words to advance his argument?

**4.** What conflict is evident in Brutus's attitude toward Cæsar? How may this conflict complicate the achievement of Cassius' goal?

**5.** Why does Cassius want Brutus's help in the conspiracy?

**6.** How does Casca's description (lines 240–255) play into Cassius' hands?

**7.** Why does Cassius stress Cæsar's physical weaknesses?

**8.** To what extent does Cassius appear to have been successful in winning Brutus over to his views? (lines 168–181; 313–317)

## STUDYING THE CHARACTERS

**9.** What evidence do you find that Antony enjoys the more relaxing activities of life and has an easygoing, optimistic outlook?

**10.** Various aspects of Cæsar's makeup are revealed in his own words and manner and in the attitudes of others toward him.

    *a.* What does Cæsar reveal about himself in the way he speaks to his wife? (lines 5–6) His directions to Antony? (lines 8–11) His dismissal of the soothsayer? (line 28) And his remarks to Antony about Cassius? (lines 204–220)

    *b.* What opinion of Cæsar is indicated by Cassius? By Casca? By Brutus? By Antony?

**11.** What quality does Brutus value most? Is he basically a man of action or of thought? What do lines 178–181 reveal about him? Why would you or would you not consider Brutus himself to be a good judge of character?

**12.** What are Cassius' motives for opposing Cæsar? What does his own description of himself (lines 77–83) reveal? What ability to judge people and events does Cassius show?

**13.** What qualities are suggested by Casca's description of the offering of the crown? What explanation does Cassius give for the change that Brutus has noted in Casca?

## VISUALIZING THE ACTING AND STAGING

**14.** What gestures might accompany these lines?

    *a.* "When Cæsar says 'do this,' it is perform'd." (line 13)

    *b.* "Fellow, come from the throng; look upon Cæsar." (line 25)

    *c.* "Why, man, he doth bestride the narrow world like a Colossus." (lines 141–142)

    *d.* "Come on my right hand, for this ear is deaf." (line 219)

    *e.* "An I had been a man of any occupation, if I would not have taken him at a word." (lines 271–272)

**15.** What example of a soliloquy is there in this scene? Why was it necessary at this point for the playwright to give us Cassius' inner thoughts?

## UNDERSTANDING AND APPRECIATING THE LINES

**16.** Cassius relates two incidents to Brutus about Cæsar to explain why Cæsar has no right to be ruler. (lines 106–134) Find two similes Cassius uses in these lines and explain why they are appropriate.

**17.** What pun does Cassius use when Brutus refers to Cæsar's having the falling sickness? What does he imply?

**18.** Cassius' statement about his plan (lines 320–327) requires interpretation.

*a.* What would you call the "writings" that Cassius intends to throw into Brutus's window that night?

*b.* People sometimes say, "She writes a good hand." What is the meaning of "in several hands" in this sentence?

*c.* What two subjects will the "writings" concern? Which will receive more stress?

*d.* What does Cassius hope to accomplish by this scheme?

## EXPLORING ISSUES OF IMPORTANCE IN HUMAN EXPERIENCE

**19.** Superstition is a universal characteristic which this play explores. What is Cassius' attitude toward the belief that the stars control men's destinies? What is your opinion of his attitude?

**20.** What indications does Cæsar give in this scene that he believes in omens or superstitions handed down by his ancestors? To what extent do people today believe in superstitions?

**21.** This scene provides further examples of the techniques used to control the mind and emotions.

*a.* To what extent does Cassius' flattery influence Brutus to consider active opposition to Cæsar?

*b.* Why does Cæsar refuse the crown when the people apparently want him to have it? Is this a smart political move? Why?

# Act I, Scene 3

## FOLLOWING THE STORY

**1.** By the end of this scene, we know that six men are definitely committed to the conspiracy against Cæsar. Who are they?

**2.** The scene ends with attention focused on Brutus. Why do the conspirators have "great need" of Brutus?

## STUDYING THE CHARACTERS

**3.** The historic Cicero was a distinguished orator, philosopher, and scholar. What criticism of Casca does Cicero imply? (lines 34–35)

**4.** Casca and Cinna react to the storm with fearful agitation, but Cassius is exhilarated by it. Why?

**5.** On what qualities in Casca does Cassius play in lines 60–87? In lines 115–118? How does Casca seem less independent in this scene than before? How does this reflect on Cassius' integrity?

**6.** Cassius recognizes Casca by his voice (line 44) and Cinna by his gait (line 137). Which quality in Cassius, already noted by Cæsar, do these two incidents illustrate?

## VISUALIZING THE ACTING AND STAGING

**7.** How might thunder and lightning have been produced on Shakespeare's stage?

**8.** The actors are more physically agitated than in previous scenes.

    *a.* What do the stage directions and Cicero's words suggest as to Casca's appearance and actions as he enters?

    *b.* How must Cassius look and act? (lines 48–55)

    *c.* What gestures might Casca use as he describes the storm?

**9.** How should the following lines be spoken? Choose the word that you feel is most appropriate.

   *a.* "You are dull, Casca, and those sparks of life
     That should be in a Roman you do want." (lines 60–61)
       (1) indulgently   (2) affectionately   (3) scornfully
       (4) gently

   *b.* "Now could I, Casca, name to thee a man
     Most like this dreadful night." (lines 75–76)
       (1) casually   (2) loudly   (3) confidingly   (4) teasingly

   *c.* " 'Tis Cæsar that you mean; is it not, Cassius?" (line 82)
       (1) naively   (2) indignantly   (3) sorrowfully
       (4) angrily

   *d.* "O Cassius if you could
     But win the noble Brutus to our party—" (lines 146–147)
       (1) regretfully   (2) reproachfully   (3) indifferently
       (4) anxiously

## UNDERSTANDING AND APPRECIATING THE LINES

**10.** Why is the ocean called "ambitious"? (line 7) Which figure of speech does this represent?

**11.** What physical details does Casca give to show that this is no natural storm? (lines 3–13, 15–28)

**12.** How does Cassius interpret these unnatural portents to achieve his own purposes? Which portent does he add? (lines 65–81)

**13.** Note the tricks of the well-skilled orator in Cassius' impassioned speeches in this scene. How does the repetition of the word "why" in lines 66–69 enhance the effect of the answer he finally gives to these questions in lines 75–81? (These are called *rhetorical questions* because no answer is really expected from the person to whom they are addressed.)

**14.** In lines 108–110 men are compared to animals. We use these metaphors today, often with the same meaning. With what qualities do you usually associate the *wolf*, the *sheep*, the *lion,* the *hind* (deer)? What is the special significance of the *lion* in this play?

**15.** Alchemy was the medieval "science" that aimed to transform base metals into gold. Express in your own words the meaning expressed by Casca in lines 163–166. What figure of speech is used?

## EXPLORING ISSUES OF IMPORTANCE IN HUMAN EXPERIENCE

**16.** Cassius' behavior brings to mind the important question of whether the end justifies the means. Note that Cassius uses deceit repeatedly—in flattering Brutus, in forging letters addressed to Brutus, and in browbeating Casca. Assuming that his cause is honorable, is Cassius justified in using deceit to further it? Why or why not?

**17.** How is Cicero's cautious remark that "men may construe things after their fashion, clean from the purpose of the things themselves" illustrated by Cassius' interpretation of the storm? In your judgment, to what extent does Cicero's remark represent a general tendency in human nature?

# Act II, Scene 1

## FOLLOWING THE STORY

**1.** Which line tells you Brutus has decided to join the conspirators? For what reason does he fear Cæsar? What evidence is there that his decision has not been an easy one?

**2.** What must be the subject of the whispered conference between Cassius and Brutus? Why is it not revealed to the audience?

**3.** In this scene Brutus three times successfully overrides the opinion of Cassius or the other conspirators. What are the three questions that are decided by Brutus's opinion?

**4.** Why does Cassius fear that Cæsar may not go to the Capitol that morning? How does Decius Brutus plan to assure his presence there?

**5.** What is the significance of the scene between Brutus and Portia so far as the plot is concerned?

**6.** What events in this scene suggest success for the conspirators? What events foreshadow immediate or eventual trouble for them?

## STUDYING THE CHARACTERS

**7.** What light is shed on Brutus's character by his treatment of his sleepy servant?

**8.** Which traits in her husband does Portia prize? What does his attitude toward her tell you about him?

**9.** How do the reactions to Brutus by the conspirators and, later, by Caius Ligarius indicate the esteem with which he was regarded?

**10.** To what extent is Brutus's refusal to take an oath (lines 119–145) proof of a quality he regarded highly in himself? Do you think the other conspirators would have preferred to take an oath? Why?

**11.** What does Brutus's reason for not wanting Cicero included in the conspiracy indicate? Do you think that Metellus Cimber's words (lines 150–155) may have also influenced his decision? Why?

**12.** The most important decision, and the only one that Cassius protests, is the proposed treatment of Antony. What do Brutus's arguments for not killing Antony along with Cæsar add to your picture of Brutus? Would you be inclined to trust Brutus's or Cassius' judgment of Antony's potential danger to their cause? Why?

**13.** Although we have seen Portia only briefly and will see her only once again, why do you feel she is someone you will remember?

**14.** Which qualities of a good leader does Brutus have? Which does he lack? Which qualities for effective leadership has Cassius displayed? What weakness has he shown? Which man, in your opinion, would make the better leader?

## VISUALIZING THE ACTING AND STAGING

**15.** How could an orchard or garden have been represented on Shakespeare's stage? What part of the stage might have served as Brutus's study?

**16.** What is wrong with the stage direction following line 199 for a play set in ancient Rome? We call such mistakes *anachronisms.* Can you find another example of an anachronism in Lucius' words in line 75?

**17.** What stage directions are implied in the lines as Portia pleads with Brutus? As Casca determines where the east lies? As Cassius introduces the conspirators?

**18.** What special costume is indicated for Ligarius? With what action might he accompany his speech in lines 333–339?

## UNDERSTANDING AND APPRECIATING THE LINES

**19.** Reread lines 21–28. Explain the metaphor in these lines.

**20.** What faulty reasoning did Brutus use in concluding that Cæsar must be assassinated?

**21.** Brutus again returns to a justification of Cæsar's death (lines 169–190), this time with an added explanation of his reasons for sparing Antony. How sound is his argument in this speech? Can men be "sacrificers, but not butchers" when they kill? Can they kill without anger? Why does Brutus wish he could kill Cæsar's spirit but "not dismember Cæsar"? Finally, what indication does he give that his purpose is to make their act "look" good rather than "be" good?

**22.** Brutus, like many of the characters of this play, was an accomplished orator. One of the special oratorical techniques was the use of carefully selected balanced opposites, often connected by such words as "not . . . but." List the examples of this technique which you find in lines 173–187.

## EXPLORING ISSUES OF IMPORTANCE IN HUMAN EXPERIENCE

**23.** You may have heard the expression, "Politics makes strange bedfellows." What does it mean? To what extent do the members of the conspiracy illustrate its truth?

**24.** Another more important fact about politics which Shakespeare explores in this play has been well expressed by an English writer, John Morley: "Those who would treat politics and morality apart will never understand one or the other." In what way is Brutus's decision to kill Cæsar an attempt to treat politics and morality apart? What great moral issue has he not faced? Can politics be completely honest and moral? What are the difficulties?

# Act II, Scene 2

## FOLLOWING THE STORY

**1.** Note the skillful way in which you are kept guessing and revising your guesses as to what Cæsar will do.

*a.* What do Cæsar's opening remarks (lines 1–6) suggest as to his state of mind?

*b.* How do Calpurnia's words (lines 8–9) contradict this assumption?

*c.* In subsequent speeches, how does Cæsar dispose of the motive which might prevent his going to the Senate?

*d.* Why does he suddenly yield to Calpurnia? Does he seem strong in his new determination?

*e.* Why does he tell Decius Brutus about Calpurnia's dream? How does Decius Brutus interpret it?

**2.** How does Cæsar's final decision end the suspense and make the climax almost inevitable?

## STUDYING THE CHARACTERS

**3.** While the hesitation and final decision of Cæsar are essential to the plot, they would be unconvincing if they did not seem to spring from his own character.

a. How is Cæsar's superstitious nature illustrated in this scene? Nevertheless, how does he show that he will sometimes interpret omens in the way that suits his own inclinations rather than being swayed by them?

b. What truth is there in his claim to fearlessness? Why does his manner of claiming it make you suspicious?

c. What traits are indicated by Cæsar's use of his name rather than "I"?

d. Note Calpurnia's remark (line 52). What would the attitude of a military man be toward overconfidence? Do you think it was the reason he yielded?

**4.** Yet, Cæsar changes his mind.

a. To what extent do you think he was moved by Decius Brutus's interpretation of the dream?

b. Which of Decius Brutus's points do you think influences Cæsar more—the implication of cowardice, or the suggestion that the Senate might offer Cæsar a crown?

**5.** How are Cæsar's gracious qualities indicated in this scene?

**6.** In what respects is Calpurnia like Portia? Unlike her?

## VISUALIZING THE ACTING AND STAGING

**7.** What evidence suggests that the storm has not ended?

**8.** What references to costume are there?

**9.** Some actresses have played Calpurnia as a nagging, neurotic wife. In your opinion, is this a valid interpretation?

**10.** This scene concludes with two *asides*. What is their purpose?

## UNDERSTANDING AND APPRECIATING THE LINES

**11.** Calpurnia's speech (lines 13–26) is the third account of the ominous events of that night. What are her additions to Casca's and Cassius' accounts?

**12.** How do the grisly details of Calpurnia's dream seem to contradict Brutus's hope that assassination can be a solemn sacrifice? Even Decius Brutus's interpretation of that dream, you will note, cannot get rid of one element in it. What is that element?

**13.** What does Cæsar mean by "Cowards die many times before their death"? (line 33)

**14.** One figure of speech which depends upon sound is *alliteration*. This is *the repetition of the same initial consonant sound in words next to or close to each other.* Note in lines 13–20 Calpurnia's use of alliteration in "fierce fiery warriors fought upon the clouds." Where in lines 43–50 does Cæsar use alliteration?

**15.** Puns are often, but not always, light-hearted. What does Brutus's grim play on the word "like" (lines 134 and 135) mean?

## EXPLORING ISSUES OF IMPORTANCE IN HUMAN EXPERIENCE

**16.** The role that fate plays in controlling human destinies fascinates all of us. But there are many disasters in life which men seem to have power to avoid yet they cannot or do not exercise that power. The Greeks said, "Whom the gods would destroy, they first made mad." What does this mean? How does Cæsar's behavior in this scene illustrate the truth of that saying?

**17.** What human instinct was Cæsar forgetting when he said it was foolish for men to fear death since it is inevitable? When had Cæsar himself, according to Cassius, displayed this instinct?

# Act II, Scene 3

## FOLLOWING THE STORY

**1.** How does Artemidorus sum up the forces ranged at this point against Cæsar? Why does he not include Publius?

## STUDYING THE CHARACTERS

**2.** What weakness of the conspirators is implied by the fact that Artemidorus knows of the conspiracy?

**3.** What opinion does Artemidorus provide of Cæsar's character? Of the character of the conspirators?

## VISUALIZING THE ACTING AND STAGING

**4.** Why must the letter be read aloud?

**5.** What stage directions does Artemidorus furnish for himself? How does this scene keep the audience informed of Cæsar's whereabouts?

## UNDERSTANDING AND APPRECIATING THE LINES

**6.** It *emulation* means *envy*, as scholars have suggested, what is the meaning of lines 12–13?

# Act II, Scene 4

## FOLLOWING THE STORY

**1.** What indications does Portia give in this scene that she knows of the conspiracy?

**2.** At the end of this act, do you feel that the confrontation between the conflicting forces is inevitable? Why?

## STUDYING THE CHARACTERS

**3.** How are Portia's feminine qualities indicated in this scene?

## VISUALIZING THE ACTING AND STAGING

**4.** Portia is extremely agitated in this scene. At which lines might she
   a. Wring her hands?
   b. Put her hands to her heart?
   c. Stand frozen in apprehension?
   d. Stagger as if about to faint?

## UNDERSTANDING AND APPRECIATING THE LINES

**5.** What statement is Portia sure that Lucius has overheard? With what words does she attempt to cover her indiscretion?

## EXPLORING ISSUES OF IMPORTANCE IN HUMAN EXPERIENCE

**6.** Portia suggests that women have more difficulty than men in keeping secrets. What is your opinion? Why?

# Act III, Scene 1

## FOLLOWING THE STORY

**1.** Shakespeare has the difficult task of making the climax, although not unexpected, a stirring and stunning event. Let us see how well he achieved this.

   a. What two chances are there that Cæsar will discover the plot in time? How is each resolved?

*b.* What final moment of suspense is there for the conspirators?

*c.* How do the conspirators contrive to get within striking distance of Cæsar? To render Cæsar's supporters ineffective? Why have they chosen as their "suit" the pardoning of Metellus Cimber's brother?

*d.* In what way do Cæsar's speeches alienate the audience?

*e.* Why are Casca's words dramatic?

*f.* Why are Cæsar's dying words dramatic?

**2.** In the first moments after a climax, especially a violent one, confusion is natural. Then, almost imperceptibly, the falling action or consequences of the climax begin to emerge.

*a.* What specific plans do the conspirators have for following up the assassination? How successful are they therefore likely to be?

*b.* How does Antony keep the attention of the audience on Cæsar?

*c.* Why does Antony pretend to make peace with Cæsar's assassins? What important concession does he win from Brutus? What does Antony later reveal as his real intention toward the conspirators?

*d.* Since Cæsar had no son, he had named a young relative, Octavius Cæsar, to succeed him. Why is Antony concerned about the coming of Octavius to Rome at this time?

**STUDYING THE CHARACTERS**

**3.** The first part of this scene provides additional insights into Cæsar's character.

*a.* When Cæsar ignores Artemidorus's letter the reason he gives is an admirable one. Why then do you find it difficult to sympathize with him?

*b.* Do you pity Cæsar as he approaches death? Why?

**4.** Antony, in the second part of the scene, gives us a different picture of Cæsar.

*a.* What adjectives does he use to describe him? What reference does he make to his achievements?

*b.* What acknowledgment of Cæsar's good qualities does he win from Brutus and Cassius?

*c.* Through whose eyes have we seen Cæsar up to now?

**5.** What is surprising about Brutus's suggestion that the conspirators bathe their hands in Cæsar's blood? What instances are there of his continued failure to understand men and events? What evidence is there of his almost naive faith in his ability to "fashion" people?

**6.** The character of Antony has been so little revealed up to this time that we are not surprised at the first report that he has fled. Note how your suspicion grows, as the scene progresses, that there is more to him than Brutus, Cassius, or even Cæsar had previously suggested.

*a.* Why did Antony send his servant rather than come himself? What evidences of good judgment do you find in the message that Antony asked his servant to convey? What does Antony's prompt arrival tell us about his whereabouts after the assassination?

*b.* How does he show his devotion to Cæsar?

*c.* Why does Antony shake the hands of the conspirators? To what conclusion does this action bring him? What word do we use to describe someone who takes advantage of any opportunity? What further indications of this quality do you find in the behavior and words of Antony?

*d.* What new qualities in Antony are shown in his soliloquy? (lines 273–294)

**7.** Which qualities in Cassius not previously indicated are shown in his reaction to Popilius Lena's remark? In his instructions (lines 100–101) to Publius? How is his keen judgment of Antony again illustrated? Why does he not insist that Antony be prevented from speaking at Cæsar's funeral?

## VISUALIZING THE ACTING AND STAGING

**8.** Note that this scene takes place in two locations What are they?

**9.** Where should Artemidorus and the Soothsayer be stationed?

**10.** Why would a dais (raised platform) and an armchair be valuable props in this scene?

**11.** Describe the movements of the conspirators, and especially of Metellus Cimber and Casca, in the moments just before the assassination.

**12.** Why are Antony and Trebonius absent?

**13.** Shakespeare's audiences liked its bloody scenes to be realistic. Bladders of pigs' blood were used. How might these have been employed to produce the gory effects of this scene?

## UNDERSTANDING AND APPRECIATING THE LINES

**14.** Identify the figure of speech in lines 65–67. Why would the North Star be known to Shakespeare's audiences?

**15.** Explain Cassius' statement in lines 111–112.

**16.** How was the action of lines 115–117 foreshadowed earlier?

**17.** Dramatic irony results when an actor's words have a deeper meaning than he is aware of. The audience, however, is aware of this. Why are lines 65–75 a good example of dramatic irony?

**18.** Explain in your own words the meaning of the following lines:

    *a.* "What touches us ourself shall be last served." (line 8)
    *b.* "Hence! wilt thou lift up Olympus?" (line 80)
    *c.* "All pity chok'd with custom of fell deeds." (line 288)

## EXPLORING ISSUES OF IMPORTANCE IN HUMAN EXPERIENCE

**19.** Movies and television programs are often criticized for their emphasis on violence and their suggestion that it is an essential, even inevitable, part of life. Shakespeare's presentation of Cæsar's assassination and its immediate effects lacks none of the blood and terror which Elizabethan audiences apparently demanded. Do you feel that Shakespeare *admired* or *condoned* violence? Find evidence for your decision in the behavior of the conspirators after the assassination; in Antony's suggestion of how violence brutalizes its perpetrators; in the assassination itself.

**20.** Which ranks higher, loyalty to one's friend, or loyalty to one's community? Brutus and Antony offer different answers to this question. What are their answers? Who do you think is right?

# Act III, Scene 2

## FOLLOWING THE STORY

**1.** In each of the following, select the answer which best completes the statement.

a. According to the evidence in lines 50–54, the one who least understood Brutus's reasons for killing Cæsar was

(1) the first citizen.  (2) the fourth.  (3) the second.
(4) the third.

b. Antony's speech indicated that Cæsar was all of the following except

(1) ambitious.  (2) valorous.  (3) generous.
(4) loyal.

c. The word "honorable" in lines 89 and 90 was probably said by Antony

(1) sarcastically.  (2) sincerely.  (3) thoughtlessly.
(4) enthusiastically.

d. In this scene we never find out

(1) what has happened to Cassius and Brutus.
(2) why Brutus allowed Antony to speak.
(3) what effect Cassius had on the crowd he addressed.
(4) what happened to Cæsar's body.

e. This scene represents the turning point of the play because

(1) Brutus makes a good impression on the crowd.
(2) Octavius, Cæsar's heir, has arrived in Rome.
(3) Cæsar is dead.
(4) Antony turns the people against the conspirators.

## STUDYING THE CHARACTERS

**2.** What errors in judgment can you find in Brutus's remarks to the crowd?

**3.** Antony, with his tricks of oratory, now dominates the scene and, for a time, the whole play. In which lines does he project these conflicting characteristics: reasonableness and unreasoning passion? tenderness and unscrupulousness? grief and humor? patriotism and personal ambition? appeals to greed and appeals to generosity?

**4.** After a study of this scene, what do you feel are the dominant traits of Antony?

**5.** How are the qualities previously exhibited by the crowd (Act I, Scenes 1 and 2) repeated and developed in this scene? What expressions of reason, sympathy, fairness, respect, and intelligence are voiced by individuals in the crowd? Why do you nevertheless doubt the deep or lasting quality of these expressions?

**6.** At what point does the crowd become a mob? How does Antony further excite the mob?

**7.** What are the good qualities that Brutus ascribes to Cæsar in his speech? Which is the only flaw he cites? What new qualities or illustrations of previously noted qualities in Cæsar does Antony give? Why is Antony's speech more convincing than Brutus's?

## VISUALIZING THE ACTING AND STAGING

**8.** In this action-packed scene, Shakespeare has given or implied numerous stage directions. What action is specified in this scene for Brutus? For Antony? For the crowd?

**9.** What action might have accompanied:

  a. "Live, Brutus! live, live!" (line 49)
  b. "Poor soul! his eyes are red as fire with weeping." (line 123)
  c. "But here's a parchment with the seal of Cæsar." (line 136)
  d. "Then make a ring about the corpse of Cæsar." (line 165)

e. "Nay, press not so upon me; stand far off." (line 174)

f. "Revenge! About! Seek! Burn! Fire! Kill! Slay!" (line 211)

**10.** The stage directions of this scene call for a pulpit. How might the dais from the preceding scene be converted for this purpose?

**11.** The most important stage property in this scene is the body of Cæsar.

a. How was Cæsar's body probably carried on stage? How must it have been covered? How might the body suggest the gory nature of the assassination?

b. The body is not only almost constantly on stage but is the focus of three significant spectacles in this scene. What effect do you think the arrival of the funeral cortege had on Brutus? On the crowd? Where might the body have been placed on stage? What is the second spectacle in which Cæsar's body is the center of attention? How might it have been borne off-stage by the mob?

**12.** Antony's oration is an actor's delight. You can share some of that delight if, after it has been read to you and by you, or interpreted by a fine actor, you study it again for its dramatic progression and pyrotechnics.

a. Why should the first twelve lines of his speech be spoken simply and sincerely, with no suggestion of irony or sarcasm?

b. After using the adjective "honorable" twice in lines 89–90, Antony repeats it six times more by line 159. How does his emphasis change with each repetition?

c. Choose, as you read the rest of this remarkable oration, the points at which he would speak softly, loudly, insistently, passionately, sarcastically, bitterly, wrathfully, tenderly, apologetically, wistfully, proudly, humbly. There are few emotions the human voice can express that Antony did not use in this scene.

**13.** Hostility to Antony is the crowd's attitude as he begins. In what lines is this attitude changed to one of mild interest? vague uneasiness? sympathy? outspoken support and anger? rage and riot?

## UNDERSTANDING AND APPRECIATING THE LINES

**14.** Whereas weapons served for words in Scene 1 of this act, words now become weapons. One man, a competent orator and respected citizen, fails, and another, who calls himself "no orator" and is reputed to be dissolute and lazy, succeeds spectacularly.

    *a.* How do the two speeches differ in *length?* What important material might Brutus have profitably included in his speech?

    *b.* How do they differ in *form?* For whom was this a possible advantage?

**15.** The speeches differ in *style.* Despite Antony's protests, he is obviously a skilled orator. He uses all the tricks of oratory that Brutus does—and a few of his own.

    a. We have referred formerly to the oratorical use of balanced sentences. The *balanced sentence* employs such expressions as: "not this . . . but that"; "if . . . then"; "as . . . so," etc. Balanced sentences are stylistic adornments which, like jewelry, are most effective when carefully selected and discreetly used. In Brutus's speech, does he make more use of balanced sentences or of natural sentences? What examples do you find of balanced sentences in Antony's oration?

    *b.* A rhetorical question is a question to which no answer is expected. It implies that there can be only one answer. Example: "Who is here so vile that will not love his country?" How many rhetorical questions are there in Brutus's speech? How many in the opening passages of Antony's speech? What effect do you think the overuse of the rhetorical question might have on an audience? Emphasis and repetition are other common devices of oratory. Which man do you think makes the more imaginative use of these techniques? Why?

**16.** Antony also made use of figurative language to secure some of his effects. Explain the figure of speech in lines 185–187. What examples of alliteration do you discover in his oration? What example of *hyperbole* (a deliberate exaggeration for emotional effect) do you find in lines 195–196?

## EXPLORING ISSUES OF IMPORTANCE IN HUMAN EXPERIENCE

**17.** One factor that a speaker must take into consideration if he is to succeed is his audience—its characteristics, interests, and attitudes. To what extent does Brutus show understanding of the crowd? How is Antony's approach to the crowd different?

**18.** Advertisers, politicians, and salesmen are well aware that most people respond readily to so-called "free" offers. How does Antony, too, show awareness of this fact?

**19.** There is probably in all of us a sentimental pleasure in seeing the "underdog" triumph. To what extent is Antony the underdog in this scene?

# Act III, Scene 3

## FOLLOWING THE STORY

**1.** What outcome of the assassination and Antony's oration is dramatized in this scene?

## VISUALIZING THE ACTING AND STAGING

**2.** What action accompanied the second citizen's reply to Cinna?

**3.** What action probably accompanied the words "Tear him, Tear him!"?

## UNDERSTANDING AND APPRECIATING THE LINES

**4.** What irony is evident in Cinna's remark in line 1, in view of his fate in this scene?

**5.** To relieve the tension of a serious or tragic scene, a dramatist often introduces elements of comedy. This is known as *comic relief.* Which lines, in your opinion, contain comic relief?

**6.** What is meant by "pluck but his name out of his heart, and turn him going"?

## EXPLORING ISSUES OF IMPORTANCE IN HUMAN EXPERIENCE

**7.** When a crowd has become a mob, Shakespeare suggests, any act, reasonable or unreasonable, may follow. Do you agree? What examples from history or contemporary events prove the truth of this?

# Act IV, Scene 1

## FOLLOWING THE STORY

**1.** After the flight of Brutus and Cassius, a triumvirate (a group of three persons sharing power) was appointed to rule Rome. Who are its members? What evidence does the scene provide of their dictatorial rule?

**2.** What rift is already apparent among the members?

**3.** What news does Antony give Octavius of the plans of Brutus and Cassius? Why does he tell it in Lepidus's absence?

**4.** Why does Octavius (lines 51–54) readily agree to follow Antony's leadership?

## STUDYING THE CHARACTERS

**5.** What new characteristics does Antony reveal in this scene?

**6.** What picture of Lepidus do we get from the testimony of Antony and Octavius?

**7.** What traits do you find in Octavius? What seems to be Antony's attitude toward him?

## VISUALIZING THE ACTING AND STAGING

**8.** This meeting historically occurred a year and a half after the assassination. For what dramatic reason did Shakespeare choose not to indicate this lapse of time?

**9.** What action is implied in lines 1–6?

## UNDERSTANDING AND APPRECIATING THE LINES

**10.** What unflattering simile does Antony employ to describe Lepidus's function? What qualities in Lepidus arouse Antony's contempt?

**11.** Which of the following adjectives does Antony's statement about Lepidus (lines 38–42) imply: imaginative, cheap, imitative, innovative, unproductive?

**12.** The metaphor in lines 51–52 requires an understanding of bear-baiting, a popular amusement of Shakespeare's time. After a bear had been chained to a post, dogs were relesed to torment him. Why is this metaphor appropriate?

**13.** What is the meaning of *levying powers*? (line 45)

## EXPLORING ISSUES OF IMPORTANCE IN HUMAN EXPERIENCE

**14.** Shakespeare implies that war makes men insensitive. Even the ties of blood mean nothing to the triumvirs. What similar examples of human callousness in wartime can you cite from history and contemporary events?

# Act IV, Scene 2

## FOLLOWING THE STORY

**1.** What apparent change has occurred in the relationship between Brutus and Cassius?

**2.** What evidence is there to suggest that a clash with the forces of the triumvirate is not far off?

## STUDYING THE CHARACTERS

**3.** To what extent does Brutus show in this scene that he can be tactful and level-headed? What former indication of this quality did you note in Act III, Scene 1, just before the assassination of Cæsar?

**4.** What evidence of Cassius' hasty temper, if any, have we had so far in the play?

## VISUALIZING THE ACTING AND STAGING

**5.** Although the scene mentions the presence of two "armies," about how many soldiers were probably needed onstage? How were the actors who played the soldiers probably used in preceding scenes?

**6.** What military equipment, costume, and stage properties might the soldiers have had? How would the leaders (generals, captains, etc.) be distinguished?

## UNDERSTANDING AND APPRECIATING THE LINES

**7.** What two possibilities does Brutus give in line 7 to explain the behavior by Cassius which has aroused his anger?

**8.** What does Brutus mean by "hollow men" (line 25)?

**9.** Up to now we have not met Brutus as a soldier. Note the military quality of the figure of speech he uses in lines 25–29. Express the meaning of these lines in your own words.

## EXPLORING ISSUES OF IMPORTANCE IN HUMAN EXPERIENCE

**10.** When Brutus says, "Wrong I mine enemies?" he is suggesting that he is certainly not wronging his friends. Which "friend" has Brutus probably forgotten when he says this to Cassius? Why is it more natural to be hurt by the wrongs done by a friend than by an enemy?

# Act IV, Scene 3

## FOLLOWING THE STORY

**1.** In each of the following, select the answer which best completes the statement.

a. Cassius is angry because Brutus
   (1) refused to send him money for his troops.
   (2) has made many mistakes in judgment.
   (3) condemned one of his followers for taking bribes.
   (4) allowed his sister to die.

b. The remark from Brutus that most enrages Cassius is
   (1) "You yourself are much condemn'd to have an itching palm."
   (2) "You wronged yourself to write in such a case."
   (3) "I am a soldier, I, older in practice, abler than yourself to make conditions."
   (4) "Fret till your proud heart break."

c. Brutus states in lines 19–29 that
   (1) all the other conspirators except him killed Cæsar for personal gain.
   (2) Cæsar was just.
   (3) Cæsar was killed because he supported those who robbed the people.
   (4) Cassius is a dog.

d. Cassius says all of the following *except*
   (1) he never denied Brutus money.
   (2) he has always had an explosive temper.
   (3) Brutus loved Cæsar more than he did Cassius.
   (4) a flatterer's eye would never see faults in a friend.

e. The famous "quarrel scene" accomplishes all but one of the following:
   (1) It leaves Brutus and Cassius enemies.

    (2) It symbolizes again the truth of Antony's prophecy in Act III, Scene 1.

    (3) It reaffirms the power of Cæsar's spirit.

    (4) It shows that quarrels would not last long if the fault was only on one side.

**2.** At the end of Act IV, do the triumvirate or the conspirators seem more likely to succeed? Why?

## STUDYING THE CHARACTERS

**3.** What inconsistency does Brutus reveal when he criticizes Cassius for not sending him money for his troops? By what means would that money have been obtained?

**4.** What new characteristics of Cassius does this scene reveal?

**5.** What opinion of Cæsar does Brutus indicate in the course of the quarrel?

**6.** Why does Brutus not tell Cassius immediately about Portia's death? Is Brutus's attitude toward this personal tragedy consistent with his character? How does Cassius' reaction differ?

**7.** What does Brutus's treatment of Lucius reveal?

**8.** What is Brutus's immediate reaction to Cæsar's ghost? Why does he awaken and question his servants? What does the appearance of the ghost reveal about the state of Brutus's mind?

## VISUALIZING THE ACTING AND STAGING

**9.** The "quarrel scene" has long been famous for its wide range of tone and atmosphere. Indicate the lines which express the following:

    *a.* hot anger
    *b.* contempt
    *c.* defiance
    *d.* threats
    *e.* humor
    *f.* warm friendship
    *g.* grief
    *h.* cool calculation
    *i.* tenderness
    *j.* fear

**10.** What kind of song did Lucius probably sing for his sorrowing master?

**11.** How do lines 301–308 help set the scene and mood for the appearance of the ghost?

## UNDERSTANDING AND APPRECIATING THE LINES

**12.** Often in this play we hear echoes or are vividly reminded of actions in earlier scenes.

    *a.* When, earlier, did a man offer wine to his friends before a fateful journey?

    *b.* Of what similar episode are you reminded when Cassius bares his breast and offers Brutus his dagger?

    *c.* How does the appearance of Cæsar's ghost carry out another of Antony's prophecies?

**13.** What does Brutus mean by "bay" in line 28? How does Cassius twist its meaning as he flings it back at him?

**14.** Why is the comparison between Brutus's temper and a "flint" appropriate?

**15.** Explain the metaphor in lines 244–247. Of what common proverbs does Brutus's speech remind you?

## EXPLORING ISSUES OF IMPORTANCE IN HUMAN EXPERIENCE

**16.** You have probably heard people say, "There's nothing like a good fight to clear the air." Do you agree? Why?

**17.** While most of Shakespeare's audience probably regarded ghosts as real, what explanation of the "appearance" of a ghost might be offered today?

# Act V, Scene 1

## FOLLOWING THE STORY

**1.** What rebuke to Antony do you find in Octavius's opening remarks?

**2.** What further evidence of dissension do you find between Octavius and Antony?

**3.** In the exchange of insults, which side seems to have the advantage? Why?

**4.** What omen has made Cassius fearful? What pessimism does Brutus exhibit concerning the coming battle? What outcome do these attitudes appear to foreshadow?

## STUDYING THE CHARACTERS

**5.** Truths (often unpleasant ones, as you have discovered in the preceding scene) come out in quarrels or at moments of fear or strain. What does this scene reveal about

    *a.* Octavius? Where does he show independence? impatience? leadership? What image does he seem to have of himself? What significance is there in the fact that both Brutus and Antony call him "Cæsar" in this scene? Do you agree with Cassius' scornful summing up of this young man?

    *b.* Antony? How is his shrewdness illustrated in this scene? Where does he demonstrate his superior ability with words?

    *c.* Brutus? Which word in Octavius's speech (lines 51–58) arouses Brutus's resentment? What is Brutus's meaning in line 60?

    *d.* Cassius? Again, in the presence of others, Cassius reproaches Brutus. What provocation in Antony's speech wrings this statement from him? Why should this enrage him more than any other charge?

**6.** Brutus has always been a Stoic. Although Stoics were permitted suicide if the evils of life threatened to destroy their spiritual or mental self-control (see the description of Portia's condition at the time of her death), Brutus blamed Cato, his father-in-law, for resorting to suicide rather than facing life. Cassius has always been a firm believer in Epicurus, the Greek philosopher who preached that a knowledge of nature freed men from superstitious fear. What cracks in the philosophy of both men are apparent in this scene?

## VISUALIZING THE ACTING AND STAGING

**7.** What action is indicated for Octavius in line 54?

**8.** The farewell scene between Cassius and Brutus is one which both men themselves suspect may be final.

  *a.* How might this be apparent in their actions and the way they speak their lines?

  *b.* Cassius practically echoes Brutus's farewell. What differences do you think there would be in the way each speaks these lines?

## UNDERSTANDING AND APPRECIATING THE LINES

**9.** What additional interpretation might there be for Octavius's statement (line 21) besides an army maneuver for those who know of the future crossing of Octavius's and Antony's paths?

**10.** Words and deeds are again the subject of discussion in this scene.

  *a.* How does Antony twist Cassius' metaphor about the bees to his own advantage? (line 38)

  *b.* To what extent is Brutus's sarcasm at Antony's expense justified? (lines 39–41)

  *c.* Which animals does Antony use in the three similes describing the assassins of Cæsar? What use did Cæsar make of one of these similes? (Act III, Scene 1, line 47) What kind of person is a "bondman"? Where in the play has that been mentioned before?

  *d.* Reread lines 78–96. What does the eagle symbolize? What kinds of birds are ravens, crows, and kites? Where in lines 78–96 does Cassius express an idea contained in line 294 of Antony's prophecy in Act III, Scene 1?

## EXPLORING ISSUES OF IMPORTANCE IN HUMAN EXPERIENCE

**11.** Many ancient Romans believed that suicide was morally defensible when a man of honor was faced with slavery or shame. Do you agree? Is it a cowardly or brave act? Why?

**12.** We have in Brutus and Cassius two men, many of whose basic attitudes and traits were completely different. Their friendship's surviving an assassination, a series of misfortunes, and a bitter quarrel may be a case of "opposites attract." If you have friends quite different from you, why have you chosen them?

## Act V, Scenes 2, 3, and 4

### FOLLOWING THE STORY

**1.** The names at the left are to be matched with the numbered identifications at the right. Not all the statements will be appropriate.

a. Brutus

b. Cassius

c. Titinius

d. Pindarus

e. Julius Cæsar

f. Messala

g. Lucilius

h. Marcus Cato

i. Antony

j. Octavius

(1) guided the sword that killed Cassius

(2) was overcome by Brutus's forces

(3) pretended to be Brutus

(4) died on his birthday

(5) was Portia's brother

(6) refused to kill Cassius

(7) was recognized as the real victor by Brutus and Cassius

(8) gave Brutus the news of Cassius' death

(9) planned Cassius' funeral in his camp

(10) crowned Cassius with a victor's wreath

**(11)** defeated Brutus's forces in the first battle

(12) was reported to have given the word for the charge too early

(13) offered amnesty to one of Brutus's lieutenants

**2.** Where in these three scenes does the final moment of suspense occur? How is it settled? Why does Brutus's defeat seem inevitable?

**3.** What elements of irony do you find in Cassius' death?

## STUDYING THE CHARACTERS

**4.** What weakness and strength of character does Cassius exhibit in Scene 3? On what other occasion did Cassius threaten to kill himself?

**5.** What new capacity of Brutus do these scenes reveal? Despite the death of Cassius and other misfortunes, what do his words in lines 1, 7, and 8 in Scene 4 indicate?

**6.** How do the attitudes of Pindarus, Titinius, Messala, and Lucilius strengthen or weaken the impressions you have formed of Cassius and Brutus?

## VISUALIZING THE ACTING AND STAGING

**7.** Cite one remark from Scene 3 by Cassius and another by Brutus that help the audience sense the presence of murdered Cæsar.

**8.** How many corpses result from the action of Scenes 3 and 4? Identify them.

## UNDERSTANDING AND APPRECIATING THE LINES

**9.** In each of the following, select the answer which best completes the statement.

    *a.* By "cold demeanor" in Scene 2, line 4, Brutus means
       (1) reluctance.
       (2) complete defeat.
       (3) pride.
       (4) humility.

    *b.* By "myself have to mine own turn'd enemy" in Scene 3, line 2, Cassius means
       (1) he has run from the battle.
       (2) he has deserted Brutus.
       (3) he has killed one of his own men.
       (4) he is war-weary.

   c. The word "spoil" in Scene 3, line 7 refers to

     (1) the fact that Brutus has spoiled Cassius' plans.

     (2) the looting of Octavius's camp by Brutus's soldiers.

     (3) the stench of war.

     (4) the waste of human lives.

   d. Titinius's cry, "Alas, thou hath misconstrued every thing" (Scene 3, line 89) shows the truth of

     (1) Cicero's remark to Casca in Act I, Scene 3, line 34.

     (2) Cassius' comparison of Cæsar with a Colossus.

     (3) Antony's prophecy.

     (4) Casca's remark as he stabbed Cæsar.

   e. All of the characters in these three scenes are glad to live or die as Romans except

     (1) Titinius.

     (2) Cassius.

     (3) Cato.

     (4) Pindarus.

   f. The words "Lest it discomfort us" in Scene 3, line 113, mean

     (1) bring physical lack of comfort.

     (2) be inconvenient.

     (3) encourage the enemy.

     (4) discourage Brutus's forces.

## EXPLORING ISSUES OF IMPORTANCE IN HUMAN EXPERIENCE

**10.** How can pessimism affect performance? Pessimists often claim that they are actually realists. Why do you, or do you not, believe this?

# Act V, Scene 5

## FOLLOWING THE STORY

**1.** What alternative does Brutus have at this point? Which does he choose? Why are you prepared for that choice?

**2.** Why do his friends refuse to help Brutus?

**3.** Why must the playwright remove all but Strato and Brutus from the scene? How does he accomplish this naturally?

**4.** How does Brutus's statement (lines 36–37) prepare for Strato's part in his suicide?

**5.** What is the significance of Brutus's dying words?

**6.** How does Antony's eulogy distinguish Brutus's motives from those of the other conspirators?

**7.** According to stage conventions, the character with the highest position delivered the last speech of the play. Why was this honor given to Octavius?

**8.** Who is the protagonist? Why did Shakespeare name his play *Julius Cæsar*?

## STUDYING THE CHARACTERS

**9.** What do the actions and words of Brutus's friends contribute to your understanding of him?

**10.** To what extent do you agree with Antony's eulogy of Brutus?

**11.** What does Octavius's immediate recruiting of Brutus's followers suggest about him? To what extent has Octavius's self-image been disturbed by Brutus's defeat of his forces? What significance is there in his announcement that Brutus's body will lie in *his* tent that night?

**12.** Antony is silent throughout this scene except when he speaks his moving eulogy of Brutus. What might his silence suggest as to his thoughts and feelings?

## VISUALIZING THE ACTING AND STAGING

**13.** Why do you think Shakespeare did not show the ghost of Cæsar appearing to Brutus at Philippi?

**14.** In this scene the playwright had the task of making Brutus's death the most moving of the three suicides in this act. How did Brutus's instructions to Strato help to accomplish this purpose? Why did he not have Brutus cover his face as Cassius had done? Why are Brutus's last lines more affecting than those of Cassius, although they relate to the same theme?

**15.** Most directors have Antony look on in awe and sorrow (sometimes weeping). Why is his silence more effective than if he had joined Octavius in talking to Brutus's followers?

## UNDERSTANDING AND APPRECIATING THE LINES

**16.** When Brutus says, "slaying is the word; It is a deed in fashion," of which deaths is he probably thinking?

**17.** What does Strato mean by "The conquerors can but make a fire of him"?

**18.** What irony would the audience recognize in Octavius's description of "this happy day" with which the play ends?

## EXPLORING ISSUES OF IMPORTANCE IN HUMAN EXPERIENCE

**19.** To the very end, Brutus remains rigidly devoted to the concepts of honor, integrity, justice, and truth. Can such a person succeed in the modern world? Why or why not?